The Gull's Way

A Sailor/Naturalist's Yarn

Dennis Puleston

VANTAGE PRESS
New York

To my many hundreds of past shipmates,
including my wonderful family

Published by Vantage Press, Inc.
516 West 34th Street, New York, New York 10001

Manufactured in the United States of America
ISBN: 0-533-11571-x

Library of Congress Catalog Card No.: 95-90440

0 9 8 7 6 5 4 3 2 1

They that go down to the sea in ships, that do business in great waters; these see the works of the Lord, and his wonders in the deep.

—Psalms 107:24

I must go down to the seas again,
To the vagrant gypsy life,
To the gull's way and the whale's way,
Where the wind's like a whetted knife.

—from Sea Fever
by John Masefield

Contents

Acknowledgments

The patience, interest and support of my family—my wife, children and grandchildren—have been essential in setting all this down in print. The encouragement of many ex-shipmates must also be acknowledged with gratitude, especially that of Navarre Macomb and Liz Scott-Graham. The latter friend also helped with the transcribing. Mrs. Violet Paczka of the Environmental Defense Fund produced a final draft of the manuscript with incredible speed and accuracy.

Introduction

Now that I have reached the venerable age of eighty-nine, I can look back on a life filled with adventure and travel. When I started out in 1931 in a small sailboat with one shipmate to satisfy my consuming desire to see the world, it seemed to be a very big planet. Pan Am had yet to shrink it by spanning the continents. It took me six years to complete the circumnavigation; now it can be done in a matter of several days. But then, Conrad Hilton was probably still in diapers and the Kentucky chicken colonel had not yet reached that exalted rank. So one of the best ways to travel on a very limited budget was by sailboat. One thus had a mobile home, with its self-contained necessities of food, water, bed, and shelter and the winds for free propulsion.

Travel then was far more of an adventure. Countries like India, China, and Australia were a very long way away for most of us. Tahiti, now one of the major airline crossroads of the South Pacific, had then no airstrip, and there was only a single small ramshackle hotel in Papeete. The population of lovely Bora Bora was limited to a small community of Polynesian fishermen and farmers. There were still naked savages of uncertain temperament in the Melanesian islands, while New Guinea, largely unexplored, was a land of mystery. World War II changed much of that. Tourism quickly followed, and air traffic proliferated. It seems to be an immutable law that the more attractive a place is, the more vulnerable it is to exploitation and degradation.

In my wanderings, my life has been many times touched by luck. Or perhaps *chance* is a better term. A chance conversation in a bar in Saint Thomas, in the U.S. Virgin Islands, brought two young Americans to see me in Tortola, and thus we first came to America; otherwise I might never have landed in the United States by way of a shipwreck in a howling gale at midnight and eventually become a U.S. citizen, with several careers awaiting me. And a chance accident in the middle of Long Island Sound, when a young girl landed in the water with a splash, caused me to meet the woman who, three years later, was to become my wife and who would be the mother of our four children.

My experiences in the Pacific islands happened to come to the attention of Rod Stephens, and I thus became involved in amphibious operations during the war. I have so often been blessed with uncommon luck in my contacts.

One such contact brought me a new career at Brookhaven National Laboratory, a government-supported nuclear sciences research installation. Reaching the mandatory retirement age of sixty-five at the end of 1970, I began a new career, back to a life at sea as a naturalist and lecturer on small cruise vessels. This latest job has enabled me to visit many of the most remote and beautiful places: the Amazon and Orinoco Rivers, the Indonesian islands, the Galápagos, the high Arctic, Alaska, Madagascar, Baja California, and Antarctica, where I have made thirty-five cruises.

Although I now see the world in far greater comfort than in those early days, I will never regret those experiences, with all their hardships and dangers. I have seen a world that is unlikely to be again, and I am indeed fortunate to have those memories.

1

Growing Up

My first love affair began when I was three, and it has continued ever since, along with a number of others. Affairs with lovely women came later. That first one was a love affair with birds. I can remember distinctly how it all began. Mother was one of twelve good Victorian children, six males, six females. Those six males were to me the world's most glamorous people. They were often coming back from far reaches of the earth. In those day, in the early 1900s, when the other side of the world seemed almost inaccesible, India, New Zealand, South Africa, and Canada were places of great romance to me.

These uncles, who must have been in their twenties or early thirties at the time, appeared frequently. One of them in particular, Alec, realized that I had a potential in me for an infatuation with wildlife and wild places. Whenever he was back he would take me out on walks, even when I was quite tiny. That first time was an experience that is probably my earliest distinct memory. He had found the nest of a song thrush, and he picked me up to look into that beautiful cup with its soft blue eggs with their black speckles. As I gazed into that little treasure chest, I could feel all the excitement emanating from him; from then on I was, to use a modern expression, turned on by birds.

But there were other love affairs. One of them was inevitable, an attraction toward boats and the sea. The little town of Leigh-on-Sea where I grew up, on the northern shore of the Thames estuary in England, was a wonderful place in which to develop one's desires and interests. It was essentially a fishing port, and it had been such for many hundreds of years. A customs report, dated 1565, describes it as "a very proper town, well furnished with good mariners, where commonly tall ships do ride. . . ." The whole Thames estuary was an area of great romance, because at that time London was one of the major shipping ports of the world. The ships would pass constantly, and I could watch them in the distance as they steamed up and down that broad channel leading to the great city. Among them were even a few square-riggers from the Baltic. And there were always fleets of the great tanned-sail barges working the tides across the flats. Near at hand was a fishing section of old Leigh, and it was here, at a very early age, that I began consorting with the local fishermen, somewhat to my parents' disapproval; the fishermen were after all a "lower class." In those days it was almost unthinkable for a boy coming from a "middle-class" family to be consorting with such "riffraff." To me, however, they represented much romance and adventure.

A very capable type of vessel had been developed for the shrimp and whitebait fisheries and for the raking of cockles on the tidal flats. This vessel, the Leigh bawley, was broad-beamed, with a well-rounded hull that would set almost upright when aground at low tide. To maintain the best speed when seining in strong winds, the mainsail could be triced up to reduce sail area or set fully, together with a topsail when the breeze was light. The fishermen would often take me along with them, and nothing pleased me more than when they let me help in handling the sails and sorting the catch. I learned much about the tides and the intricate channels between the flats; with an average tidal range of eighteen feet, there were miles of sandbars and creeks exposed at low tide. It was then that with short-handled rakes we could gather cockles, taking care always to retain enough water around the beds to loosen the sand where the little mollusks were buried. Then, with a flooding tide, we motored up Leigh Creek to the cockle sheds, where the catch was washed, steamed, and separated from the shells. Years later, I learned that these fine men had responded to the urgent call for vessels to evacuate the defeated British troops from the beaches at Dunkirk during some of the darkest days of World War II and several of them lost their lives in this gallant operation.

So it was only a matter of time and cash before I owned my own craft. She was a sturdy but leaky old row-boat, but she was my first command and I loved her. I borrowed paint and fixed her up, named her *Gannet*, and ventured out. I was following that classic dictum of the water rat in *The Wind in the Willows* when he stated that "there's nothing quite so nice as simply messing about in boats." As soon as I felt she was seaworthy, I began exploring the creeks between the salt marshes, where redshanks, oystercatchers, lapwings, curlews, and other exciting birds lived. Thus, I was able even at that early age to combine those two love affairs, birds and the sea.

But one is never quite satisfied in the pursuit of romance. As Conrad very aptly said: "Romance is always just over the horizon"; and as I grew up, of course, I wanted to venture farther and farther. Father had a comfortable, sturdy sailing dinghy, and it was on this that I first mastered some of the arts of sailing, and from then on I had to have a sailboat. When I reached my teens, this came to pass. At first my boats were rather small apologies for overnight cruising, but I didn't mind the lack of comfort in sleeping on the ribs of a small boat. Several of us did eventually cross the five-mile span of the estuary and landed on the Kent shore, feeling rather like Columbus or Pizarro. That, however, did not satisfy us for long. We wanted a cruising boat.

In addition to actually sailing boats, my interest was further inflamed by reading what little literature there was at that time on long-distance small-boat cruising. Joshua Slocum had already circumnavigated the world, and his tale of the voyage of the *Spray* had me enthralled. Then there was Mulhauser, with the *Amaryllis*, who also circumnavigated the world, enduring many hardships. There were not many others, but the one that made the deepest impression was the author of a small novel titled *The Riddle of the Sands*. This was the story of a small-boat man who cruised in the type of waters where we did our cruising, the tidal flats and winding channels on the east coast of Britain and along the coasts of northern Germany and behind the Frisian Islands. This author was Erskine Childers, a man who had obviously done a great deal of cruising in these challenging waters and had a thorough knowledge of them. Regrettably, he became allied with the Irish rebels and was eventually executed by the British as a spy. But his book is still a bible among small-boat sailors, particularly those who cruise in the waterways and among the sandbars of the North Sea.

We had a friend, somewhat older than ourselves, who had a cruising boat. Albeit she was only fourteen feet long, wonder of wonders, she had a cabin, she had a Primus stove, and therefore she was a floating home. On this we could venture farther afield, and eventually we did "go foreign." By that I mean we were able to venture over to the Continent, to some of the ports along the English Channel, and into the North Sea, to France, Belgium, and Holland.

But these adventures came after the intervention of World War I in 1914–18. To a boy around the age of ten it was difficult to take those terrible years too seriously. I did not appreciate the misery of our troops, suffering the hardships of trench warfare, with its mass slaughter interspersed with long periods of inaction in muddy, rat-infested dugouts. The late Victorian and Edwardian ages had spawned a breed of comfort-loving people. From their cricket and croquet matches and afternoon teas on the greensward they were brutally dumped into the shell-torn wastes of Flanders, to die on barbed wire or choke on poison gas. To me, this was a period of great excitement, and living as we did at the mouth of the Thames, I often had the opportunity to witness some of the action.

The Germans, in what now seems a ridiculously futile effort, tried to cow the British population by bombing. In those days bombing consisted of picking up a small metal object and tossing it over the side of a cockpit, hoping it would fall somewhere near human activities. London of course was a target; and as we built up our defenses against these aerial attacks, the mouth of the Thames became a bastion for aerial defense. There was even a huge searchlight at the end of our road.

The first German attacks came by way of zeppelins, those great hydrogen-filled sausages that were extremely vulnerable. I distinctly remember being called out from under the kitchen table, where we were told by the authorities to take shelter during blackouts, and standing in the street to see these great flaming objects coming down behind our town. It was so easy for our fighter pilots to fly above them and drop small incendiary bombs on them. So very quickly in the game the Germans abandoned these clumsy, slow-moving, vulnerable objects and resorted to airplanes, slowly becoming more sophisticated, and eventually to the twin-engine Gothas.

At that time Mother and Father, regardless of war, had to take their summer holidays. Mother's youngest sister, Winifred, was asked to baby-sit for us: two boys and two much younger girls. Winifred, somewhat reluctantly, I presume, agreed to do this. Even to this day, I shudder to think of what we put that poor lady through.

There was one very dramatic attempt by the German Gothas to penetrate our aerial defenses and mount a huge daylight raid on London. Behind Leigh there was a military airport. The fighters came up and, in those days of slow, small aerial craft, one could watch the dogfights with fascination: planes coming down in flames, attacks, dodgings, and all the excitement of following a fairly slow-moving aerial battle on a large scale. My brother, Ronald, two years older than I, said, "Let's go out and watch." So we dashed out into the street and went up to the top of the road where we could have a better view of all the thrills of this great spectacle. In the meantime, with all the explosions taking place, Winifred was becoming more and more frantic. To this day I regret the agonies of apprehension I must have given her, but of course Ronald and I were careless of such things at our tender age, and to us this battle was one of the greatest thrills of World War I.

I have other memories of that period. I can remember actually hearing from far away the booming of the guns on the continent. Another day we could tell when there was a great offensive underway by the crowing of the cock pheasants. These birds were very sensitive to the distant rumblings, and they crowed more than ever.

To imply that my parents routinely abandoned their children would be absolutely incorrect. They were loving parents. My father, somewhat reticent, was unable to demonstrate his affections. But my mother was a most demonstrably loving person. She was also extremely talented. In those days of miniatures, she was a highly recognized portrait painter. These tiny miniatures of one's beloveds would be fitted into lockets to be worn on a chain around the neck. She would perhaps spend several weeks painting one tiny face on an oval of ivory. She very soon saw that I had artistic interests and encouraged me in every way she could, which was not at all difficult. And although I was much more interested in painting birds and mammals than human faces, I very quickly developed a desire, which has remained with me all my life, to record with watercolor what I see in the wild places of the world.

I can understand my parents' desire to get away by themselves sometimes, and that is why they took an annual two-week holiday on the south coast of England, where Mother could relax and sketch. But aside from these absences, we always traveled as a family. The creeks that wound through the salt marshes that we could explore with the sailing dinghy and the lush meadows around Leigh were perfect places for picnics and blackberry and mushroom gathering. And then Father entered the modern age by buying a car, and we could venture farther afield. The county of Essex in those days had much beautiful rural coutryside; it was noted for its towering elms, prosperous farmlands, and charming villages. This was a very pleasant environment in which to

7

grow up, especially in the atmosphere of close and loving parents, who encouraged me in my varied interests.

In retrospect, one area we, like all Victorian and Edwardian families, were sadly lacking was in any discussion of the sacred subject of sex. Pregnancy was never referred to. To hide her pregnancy, the woman would wear clothing so voluminous no one could possibly suspect she was carrying a child. When my two sisters were about to be born, the secret was so inviolable that my father arranged for me to go on walking tours to places like Scotland and southwest England so that Ronald and I would know nothing about it. And by the time we got home, there would be our two baby sisters. This all seems highly ridiculous in these days, and my mother once confided to me that up to the time of her marriage she had a vague idea that babies somehow emerged from the navel.

So I got my sex education from that very productive but often inaccurate source, the gutter. Boys of my own age perhaps knew little more than I did and whispered about these strange, almost incomprehensible mysteries, which somehow didn't boggle my mind too much. I was thinking too much about other matters. But I do remember reaching the stage when I wanted to have pet rabbits, and the fellow from whom I bought this pair of rabbits explained to me the difference between a male and a female. I, in my innocence, believed this was a peculiarity of rabbits: that the male had a tiny appendage, which one could find by parting the fur in the animal's stomach, and the female had a tiny aperture the male did not have. I remember recounting these peculiar phenomena to another friend and having him burst into laughter, which left me completely baffled. Perhaps we have gone overboard in these days of frank discussions of sex; certainly all of the mysteries have gone. But there must be virtually nobody anymore who can claim that he was able to grow up in perfect innocence of this very vital area of information.

As I entered my early teens I experienced without question the most miserable era in my life, although quite a short one. Heretofore, I had attended a local day school, an excellent one. But to proceed further in my education it was decided that I should be sent away to a boarding school.

Saint Lawrence College, in the back of Ramsgate in the county of Kent, had a splendid reputation. I have no criticism of the quality of the education it gave its pupils. The professors were top-notch, dedicated teachers. They worked us hard and their courses were stimulating. Relations with fellow students, however, were another matter. Anyone who has read *Tom Brown's School Days*, that great classic of British education, will remember the brutalities that existed between seniors and newcomers. This was just part of the system. The seniors had a completely free hand to inflict upon the new boys any kind of humiliation and physical torture they had in mind. Any sign of rebellion would quickly result in the infliction of further degrading experience on the victim. Perhaps one of the most degrading experiences was a practice called "new boy's concert."

About a week after we had arrived at school the seniors decided that any sign of what was known as lip, in other words any indication that one was halfway satisfied with himself, should be repressed at all cost. A very ingenious form of humiliation had been designed, and this involved having to stand on a desk and sing while one's own new books, of which one was naturally very proud, were used as ammunition. If the wretched student was

9

so paralyzed with terror and embarrassment that he was speechless, he would be tormented much more. The only hope was to gasp out in trembling voice whatever few words of some song one could remember, and hope that one could pick up one's books afterward without too many missing pages and broken bindings. This was the ultimate torment, but there were many others.

One other form of humiliation was "running the gauntlet." This required the victim to run between the two ranks of the seniors, each armed with a knotted towel, with which to get in as many swats as possible as the victim ran by. A variation of this required the victim to crawl under the row of beds in one of the seniors' dormitories, being swatted while in the gaps between the beds.

For juniors considered by the seniors to be particularly in need of discipline, an especially brutal form of torment was designed. This required the victim to hold his head underwater in a washbasin while being swatted on the behind. If he brought up his head for air before the beating was over, he was forced to submerge again.

For the first year one was considered as some kind of inferior form of scum, which must be kept in its place. Walking down a corridor as a senior approached, one was required to stand with one's back against the wall until the senior had passed. The fagging system involved running to a cry of "Fag!" to find out what some senior wanted done. Maybe to oil his hockey stick or cricket bat, maybe to polish his shoes, maybe to wash out some underwear, but it was usually the last fag to arrive that was given the assignment. This is a form of slavery, as were all other forms of repression that were ignored by the school administration. Even in my short experience at this school, several boys who couldn't take it anymore ran away. Nobody ever complained to the school administration or their parents back home; that would have been a sign of weakness and effeminacy that was unthinkable. So we gritted our teeth and endured all of this, and eventually, as we became seniors, we also became petty sadists or we just ignored the whole system. Perhaps I can take a certain amount of pride in having refused to go along with this futile form of self-gratification, which, obviously, added nothing to the dignity of the seniors who practiced these forms of torture.

In spite of all this, I found a certain amount of pleasure in schooling. Partly, of course, by the excellent teaching we received, and also, as I regained a modicum of self-esteem after all the humiliation, I began to realize that this particular part of Kent was a paradise for wildlife. I found several friends who felt the same way as I did, and with bicycles we were able to explore the nearby Romney marshes.

These marshes were a great source of interest to me, particularly during the winter months. Here swarms of shorebirds (sandpipers, plovers, and their kin) assembled, and from then on I was particularly enamored of them. Most of them breed far to the north in the Arctic tundra and from there make their remarkable migrations, not only to the shores and marshes of Britain, but to lands far to the south. As I was to find subsequently, they even navigate their way, by means that are wonderful and mysterious to us, to small islands in the vast expanses of the Pacific and Indian Oceans. The eloquent nature writer Peter Matthiessen calls them the Wind Birds and this is an appropriate name for them, for they live and travel by the wind. Their plaintive calls remind one of windswept shorelines, rolling heathlands, and desolate swamps. Yet in spite of the rigors of their journeys

11

and their stressful lives, they always appear to be in perfect condition, their intricately patterned plumage immaculate. These birds are the ultimate embodiment of nature's most perfect heavier-than-air flying mechanism, and they have always captured my special admiration.

We started a natural history club at school and began to build up a collection of specimens—butterflies and moths, shells, pressed flowers, feathers, and rocks. We taught ourselves taxidermy; in the Ramsgate butcher shops we sometimes found waterfowl hanging up with the sides of beef, and if they were not too badly mangled and we could afford it, they ended up as stuffed and mounted specimens. I remember a drake red-breasted merganser (though who would want to eat such a fishy duck?) of which I was particularly proud. And somehow one young naturalist managed to smuggle a .22-caliber rifle into school. Using dust shot, several house sparrows and starlings were added to our "museum," an unused building behind the main school complex. Fired with ambition, we even started compiling a book on the local bird-life; it ran to about thirty pages before our energies were diverted elsewhere.

Besides the humilations, another unpleasant aspect of Saint Lawrence College was the food. By modern standards it was, to be simply stated: inedible. Breakfast consisted of a bun with a few currants in it and cocoa without milk or sugar. The midday meal was usually a slab of very poor meat with boiled cabbage, in which one could find quite large caterpillars that had, regrettably, met their end in the cooking pot. Supper consisted of another bun, and perhaps a bowl of oatmeal without milk or sugar and plentifully filled with large, soggy lumps and unidentified black spots.

So at this time, when our bodies were developing to their maximum extent, we were in a constant state of ravenous hunger. There was a system whereby one was able to supplement this dreadful food by bringing from home what was known as a tuck box. This was usually a small wooden chest in which were stored cans of condensed milk, bags of candies, and cookies. Condensed milk was one of the great luxuries. With two holes punched in the can we could suck at it, pulling out this thick, creamy glop. But usually the tuck boxes were soon emptied. There was also, if one had pocket money, a tuck shop where one could buy toffees, toffee apples, and a few other items. But for this one needed pocket money, and pocket money was hard to come by; usually it was in short supply for most of us. Somehow we survived all this, but I can still remember the gnawing hunger and the visions of delectable food floating in front of us, as we sat in our classes.

On the rare occasions when pocket money was available, we somehow managed to smuggle food bought in the Ramsgate shops for a dormitory feast after lights out, known as a "dorm gut." It was probably the secrecy and illegality that gave these feasts their additional glamor. The fact that we had to eat in the dark and talk in whispers did not add to the comfort. Some of the combinations were rather revolting; sausages smothered in jam were popular, and I recall once, on a dare, consuming six chocolate eclairs, each crowned by an oily sardine. But someone topped this record by downing eight.

Saint Lawrence, however, was surely no worse than any other of the fine colleges in Britain at that time. It was all part of the somewhat bizarre attitude that this kind of thing toughened one up, the same kind of attitude one finds, to a great extent, in reading about the early polar expeditions, particularly the British ones, where everything was done in what is known as the hard way. This was to show our great fortitude and endurance. Perhaps in some cases it helped. I know it helped me subsequently, when I had to live those six years while cruising in remote parts of the world on a very limited budget, where foods were very scarce and often of inferior quality. Now that I live comparatively in the ultimate lap of luxury, I appreciate it to the fullest. I doubt if one could ever fault me for complaining about food these days. I love it all.

After the first year, life became much more tolerable, in spite of the poor food. I began to enjoy the sports: cricket and swimming in the summer, field hockey and football (soccer) in the winter. Long-distance running was of special appeal to me, and table tennis (Ping-Pong) could be played in the common rooms. There were also tricks that could be played on one's schoolmates.

The latrine system lent itself to a sadistic form of sport known as "fireboating." There was a row of ten cubicles served by a flushing arrangement in a single gutter running under the seats in all the cubicles. The trickster based himself in the upstream cubicle, ready with a boat made of newspaper. Then, when the automatic system flushed, the fireboat was lit and launched, to be borne downstream by the current, under the bared bottoms of the unfortunates in the other cubicles. The trickster, in the meantime, vacated his cubicle, assuming innocence as he listened to the indignant howls of his victims.

Another trick, usually practiced near a term's end, was designd to finish off the contents of half-empty toothpaste tubes. In front of the main building, a mock fight was started, and at once heads popped out of windows to watch. The plotters on the top floor, armed with tooth-paste tubes, attempted to squeeze long ribbons of sticky paste on the heads protruding from the windows below. Anyone turning his head upward would receive the mess right in the face.

Following my graduation from Saint Lawrence the rest of my education flowed along in far easier fashion. I no longer boarded out and, therefore, had no more humiliation and was able to eat acceptable food. Also, this gave me more opportunity for "messing about with boats."

My first cruise overseas was memorable in that it was very poorly planned, so we ran into trouble with the authorities. The two of us set out in a sixteen-foot cutter and sailed over to Gravelines on the French coast. But in our ignorance, full of pride in our exciting passage, we were soon confronted by the gendarmes, who began questioning us, demanding papers we did not have, and so we were ordered back to our vessel. Long communications must have ensued between the local gendarmes and the higher-level authorities, perhaps as far away as Paris. But eventually it was decided that we had committed an unpardonable act in entering their country without the proper papers. So from then on a guard was required to keep an eye on us and our vessel, to make sure we did not make another landing.

The weather turned bad, as it so often does in the North Sea. Rain and gales came one after another, and the wretched guards had to crouch down in the lee of a bank, as best they could, to perform their most unexciting duties. We were reasonably comfortable on board, and we had brought along with us an enormous supply of kippers, wrapped in newspaper. Also, we were able to collect enough rain in a few pots and pans to give us sufficient water for drinking and for cooking our kippers. This was perhaps a tribute to this noble fish, that in spite of living on them and nothing else for five days I still enjoy a well-smoked kipper. By the end of five days, however, our kippers were almost all gone, and in spite of the still-persistent gale we realized that it was time to leave. Fortunately, the wind had swung around from the northwest to the southeast, which gave us a following wind. Reefing the main down as far as it would go and using a pocket handkerchief of a storm jib, while towing our dinghy on a long double painter, we got under way. At this juncture the guard onshore became convinced that we were setting out for our doom, for it was still blowing a full gale. He began running along the bank, waving his arms, crying, demanding us to return to the shelter of the harbor. But we had decided to leave and thus we had a very exciting passage, but we did make it back.

In spite of the poor planning that had gone into this particular voyage, we were extremely proud of ourselves, and we had learned an important lesson: that safety at sea has nothing much to do with the size of the vessel, but a very small vessel, if well found, well equipped, and well handled, will go through quite as much as many a far larger craft. From then on we were able, whenever we had the time, to make further cruises to the Continent. Subsequently, of course, they were planned far better, and with the paperwork necessary to enable us to be received by the local officials under the proper auspices.

It was on one of these subsequent cruises that I had my first experience with the demon sex. There were four of us cruising the Netherlands that summer, and we were having an idyllic trip through the canals of this lovely little country. We had anchored alongside a seawall and were preparing the evening meal, which as usual consisted of boiled kippers, when along the bank came two young Dutch girls on bicycles. They were typically Dutch, somewhat plump, neat-looking, and wildly attractive to all of us. They stopped to look, and we looked at them, and we invited them to come aboard. They seemed to be quite ready to do so. So I rowed over and we got them onto the ship, with which they were very intrigued. Although I could speak no Dutch, I was able to communicate with them in sign language, and found that they worked in a glue factory, certainly not the most romantic background. Nevertheless, they were to us wildly attractive—in fact, one might say voluptuous.

The end of it was that one young lady remained on board and I took the other one off in the rowboat for a "row." We landed on a grassy seawall, and that's where I found out about girls. It was an odd place for a romance, but it was a nice evening, and she was more than cooperative. A good time was had by both of us, and I decided that sex was a very pleasant addition to sailing. From then on, I suppose, I had many of the attributes of the traditional sailor out for a spree when he gets ashore. Be that as it may, I managed to stay out of trouble, and I sincerely hope that the few young maidens with whom I was able to establish a relationship also managed to avoid any particular problems. Speaking of the combination of sex and sailing, I must admit that I was somewhat inflamed by the descriptions of the South Sea island maidens and their easy accessibility. Although I was not prepared to admit it at the time, it may have been one of the factors in inspiring me to consider the possibility of sailing to those romantic islands.

There were, however, a number of other incentives; Conrad was still beckoning. In fact, his beckonings were more emphatic than ever. By this time I had completed my education (it was the late twenties) and taken a job in the City of London, thirty-odd miles away, so as to be self-supporting. As jobs went, it was interesting, and it kept me out of doors. I was what is known as a runner for Barclays Overseas Bank. This involved taking shipping documents to the offices of the consignees and obtaining from them some kind of commitment to pay for the shipment that was coming to them. It also involved exploring many tiny alleyways, climbing stairs into musty old offices, and handling shipping documents covering all kinds of exotic freight from many parts of the world, such as ivory nuts from the Congo, spices from the East Indies, rum from Barbados, and many other fascinating cargoes. But London was still a city, and I was walking on pavements, which I abhorred. But in the meantime, I became more dedicated to the job, for a very definite reason.

I had already taken a number of cruises with a friend, Geoff Owen, when we both discovered one evening that we had the same dream. As I recall, we were sitting on a seawall, having just completed a weekend cruise in a small boat, and were watching the ships heading out of the river on the ebbing tide. One passed by, obviously a fruit boat, and I turned around to Geoff and said, "I wish I was heading where she was," because I knew she was bound for the tropics. Then he turned to me and said quietly, "I was just thinking the same thing." From that point on we began sharing our dreams. This culminated in the decision to devote all our efforts toward a time when we could have the kind of ship we wanted and could head off into the blue, with our ultimate objective the tropical seas and their islands. We both had jobs in London; we both had plenty of experience in sailing, and we had been through some rough cruises together. All we needed was some more studies and sufficient money to see us at least on the first few legs of our voyage.

2

Setting Off to Sea

It took Geoff and me about five years to gather sufficient funds for the kind of vessel we wanted. *Uldra*, named after a Norwegian spirit of the forests, was a stout little ship, twenty-nine feet long, drawing five and a half feet of water. She was built in 1905, my own birth year, of teak and kauri pine, well equipped, originally rigged as a cutter. But we did not like the idea of her boom overhanging the stern. So we cut down the boom and installed a tiny mizzen right on the transom, thus bringing the mainsail inboard, in case we needed to take in sail in heavy weather. We had tried her out under very adverse conditions in the English Channel during a full gale, having rounded Land's End with wind velocities of sixty-three miles an hour recorded on shore. So we knew she could take it. She was by modern standards an old-fashioned gaff-rigged-mainsail type of craft; she did not have a high or hollow Marconi mast, instead a stout solid spar of Sitka spruce; her sails were tanned and so they were impervious to weather; and as far as we were concerned, she was in every way a perfect ship. We were to find out later a few of her deficiencies, the main one being her lack of an auxiliary engine, which made coming alongside a dock a rather tricky maneuver and, in the case of entering passes into coral lagoons, with their almost constant strong head currents, a very dangerous and perhaps foolhardy procedure.

In any case, she was a fine ship to start out on. By this time it was 1931. I had taken a course in practical celestial navigation, because, although we were perfectly familiar with coastwise navigation, neither of us had ever had experience at sea of shooting the sun, taking a chronometer reading at the same time, and calculating our latitude and longitude by consulting the right tables. But we felt sure that we could master this abstruse art quite easily. Although neither of us had mastered the theory of celestial navigation as expounded in a massive tome like Bowditch, we at least knew how to use a sextant and which tables to refer to when making our calculations. This is all we really needed; the theory could be studied later. So we sailed out of Leigh and down the Channel, stopping at several ports before we made our final departure from our homeland.

Before we sailed we were careful to ensure that we had sufficient supplies to last us for at least six months. We had an extensive supply of canned goods, which we stowed under the bunks on either side of the main cabin. We had airtight canisters in which we stowed some of the staples, like flour, lentils, dried peas, rice, sugar, cornmeal, and oatmeal. We also had about forty-five pounds in cash, which seems like very little these days, but then it was the equivalent of almost $120, and with care we would be able to last out for quite a while. We had already made arrangements with several sailing and travel magazines to publish articles we wrote describing our experiences on our voyage. And so we did have the prospect of a future income, although it would obviously be quite a small one. As for water, we had a tank with a capacity of 120 gallons. With careful use, this would last us a long time; we would use seawater for washing dishes and clothes. And we even made it a practice to dip our toothbrushes over the side rather than using fresh water.

Having already bid farewell to my dubious family, wondering when we would see them again, eventually Geoff and I reached Falmouth. This was the period of the equinoctial storms in the latter part of September, and we knew we might very well encounter bad weather as we headed southward toward the coast of Africa to pick up the trade winds. But we knew we must get away soon. So we took our last farewell glance at the land, wondering when and if we would ever see it again as it disappeared in a rain squall. We laid a southerly course to round the northwest tip of France and headed down toward the Bay of Biscay, which is notorious for its westerly gales.

As we drew farther away from land the seas began slopping over into the cockpit, and very soon we could hear water sloshing around in the cabin. While I handled the tiller, Geoff went below to work the semirotary pump handle, to clear the bilges. After a few strokes of the pump handle, the flow of water stopped, and we realized that something was jamming the intake. This involved straddling the floorboards, pulling them up, and groping around in the bilge for the intake to the pump. Geoff found a few scraps of paper that had somehow been sucked against the intake, and muttering a few seaman-like oaths, he cleared the intake, reinstalled the floorboards, and again started to pump. But again after a few strokes the pump refused to suck. So again this involved groping in the bilges for the intake. After this happened several times, Geoff, in his frustration, began looking at these pieces of paper, wondering where they were coming from. He looked at one and saw the word *beans*, and then he realized what had happened. We had thoughtlessly stowed all our canned goods under the bunks on either side of the cabin. But with the violent rolling of the ship the bilge water had washed off all our labels. From then on mealtimes became somewhat interesting, since we were never sure whether we were opening a can to find beets, peaches, or some other unexpected but nevertheless edible provision. This made meals a little complicated, but at least it taught us our first lesson: in the future remove all paper labels from cans and paint symbols indicating their contents.

A couple of days later we ran into calmer weather farther south in the Bay of Biscay, and from then on we had pleasant conditions, until by dead reckoning we realized we must be somewhere close to the coast of northwest Spain. So with a self-conscious fanfare, I brought out the sextant, Geoff manned the chronometer, I took a sight of the late-afternoon sun, and just as I got my reading I shouted down to Geoff, so that he could record the Greenwich mean time. Then I began my calculations —somewhat laboriously, it must be admitted. But eventually I came up with a position that, to my surprise, put us some five thousand feet up in the Pyrenees Mountains. Surely Europe could not have sunk; it is a pretty large body of land. Perhaps I had made a mistake in my calculations, so I went very carefully through all my figures again, checking the right tables, and then discovered I had added where I should have subtracted, which put us some twelve miles off Cape Finisterre. Just then Geoff called down to me, "Hey, I can see land and a lighthouse ahead of us!"

Well, sure enough, this was Cape Finisterre, and we had our first manifestation of the black magic of measuring the angle of the sun, looking up the right tables, and doing the right things with the right numbers, so one can find out one's position at sea. And surely that is a form of black magic, if one is not familiar with the whole theory behind it. From then on we never had any trouble with our navigation, and for a small slow-moving boat such as ours, with the tropics almost always providing us with good conditions for making our celestial observations, it became easier and easier as time went on. Now, of course, modern navigators have no need for instruments like sextants and chronometers. With satellite navigation the only thing you need is to look over your chart table and there is your latitude and longitude spelled out on an instrument every few minutes as your position changes. Perhaps that has taken some of the romance out of it, but one must admit it is certainly handy.

Our first foreign port on this memorable adventure was the little Spanish sardine-fishing village of Corcubion, tucked away under Cape Finisterre, with a steep mountain in the background, covered with heather that was somehow more remindful of Scotland than of Spain. We drifted into this lovely harbor in the late afternoon, and soon a curious fisherman came alongside and offered us some sardines. We indicated in a combination of broken Spanish and sign language that we needed clearance before going ashore, and to our surprise this friendly fisherman tapped his head as if the port captain was somewhat addled in the brain. We thought this rather strange, but nevertheless our friend offered to lead us to *el capitán del puerto*. So he ferried us ashore with our papers and we wandered through the streets. Everyone we met went through the same gestures, pointing to their heads, and we began to wonder whether the port captain was dangerous or simply senile. Very soon the whole matter was cleared up when we reached what was obviously a barbershop, for we then realized that the port captain was having a shave and a haircut. We entered, and after a rapid introduction by our kindly guide, the port captain rose to his feet in midshave, and draped as he was in a voluminous towel rather like a Roman senatorial toga, he went into a flowery speech of welcome. The friendliness of this little town was a delight, and we were tempted to remain there feeding on free sardines, which were generously offered by every vessel that passed us.

But we realized that we must continue on, so after several days we sailed south to Vigo, a much larger port farther along the west coast. Here we received hospitality from the local yacht club, and we were even invited to a dance. This was something we had not anticipated, and in our somewhat shoddy and inadequate clothing we felt a little out of place. But at least we thought this might be a good opportunity to come to close quarters with some of the beautiful señoritas. That was all very well, but each señorita was guarded by an older dowager, and Geoff and I found that trying to establish intimate relations with the señoritas was out of the question, because the dowagers would never let them out of their sight. This became so frustrating that we gave up early in the game. To see these beauties, displayed in all their tempting finery and yet utterly inaccessible to us, was more than we could endure, so we soon faded out and headed on for Madeira.

Even in those days Madeira was a favorite port for tourist ships, and this had resulted in an enormous fleet of bumboats, manned by salesmen who were ready, the minute we anchored, to tempt us with many items that were totally useless to us. One bumboat was overloaded with enormous wicker chairs, and how the salesman could calculate these monstrosities would fit into our cabin was beyond our comprehension. Then there was a salesman of six-foot-tall potted palms. Another came close, somewhat secretively, and whispered that he knew of a very attractive German lady in a nearby hotel.

I soon made a striking discovery that applies not only to Madeira but to many Mediterranean ports. We noticed that all of the bumboats had flanges attached to their oars with pins going through those flanges, so that the oars could be released without having them slide into the sea. Then we realized the necessity for this arrangement, because no Latin bumboat man could possibly talk without using both of his hands. The idea is to release your grip on the oars and rise to your feet and speak with many violent arm and hand movements. If you were unable to do this, if you had to hang onto your oars, for instance, you would be speechless.

We did not stay in Madeira too long. It is a lovely island, wine was cheap, but it was too popular with the big cruise ships and there were too many touts and vendors for our liking, so we headed on for the Canary Islands.

In reading of past voyages of exploration, we had again and again come across descriptions of the horrors of scurvy, resulting from the lack of vitamin C. We were determined that we would take steps to avoid such a disaster. The Canaries are great producers of many kinds of fruit, and I knew that oranges were a rich source of vitamin C. We did take one bag of oranges, but we decided to stock up mostly on green bananas that would ripen one by one as we made the crossing of the Atlantic. So we bought two huge complete sticks of green bananas. They took up most of our cabin space, so we had to crawl over them to get into our bunks, but we looked forward with great anticipation to the ripening of the fruit.

We stayed in Tenerife for about a week while we made our final preparations for what would be for us a historic passage, some three thousand miles of open ocean with no land until we reached the islands of the Caribbean. When we finally took off and began marking off our daily noon positions on the chart, it seemed as if we would never cross that vast expanse of open ocean. We saw El Pico, the great conical peak on Tenerife, for several days, and we must have been a good ninety miles away while it was still in view. But we soon settled down to a routine on board, the trade winds freshened, and we began to enjoy our passage. This was early October, the same time of year that Columbus had made his historic crossing in these latitudes. He, in a moment of poetic inspiration, described it as "lacking nothing but the song of nightingales to be remindful of spring in Andalusia." The old navigator was correct. It was idyllic. The trade winds blew fresh and steady from the east, and on our westerly course we had a following wind and sea. Under these conditions, we had no spray coming on board, so we could have the hatch and skylight open and could air out our bedding when needed.

We had designed a twin square-sail rig that consisted of a double yard, one yard on either side of the mast, with each yard set independently of the other. So even with the mainsail set on one quarter we could still set the square sail cocked well forward on the windward side. With the wind steadily behind us we did not need the mainsail at all but just ran under these two square sails, thus eliminating the dangers of jibing the mainsail, which is a great worry with a following wind. We set the tiny mizzen and sheeted it in flat, which succeeded in damping the roll to some extent. So the ship remained fairly steady as we began reeling off between a hundred and a hundred and twenty miles a day as we headed westward.

Each day we looked carefully at our bananas to see when the first one ripened. After about a week we were delighted to see that one had turned a bright yellow. We brought it on deck and solemnly and carefully divided it in two and ate it with much relish. The following day we had a banana apiece. The third day we were beginning to think of banana recipes such as hashed with a little condensed milk, sliced, fried, and other ways of making them more interesting. But we were soon confronted with a terrible problem: the bananas were engulfed in a kind of haze, for the fruit flies had emerged and they were there in the millions. When one of us lay down to take a rest, the fruit flies joyously explored every aperture they could find on our bodies. After a few days of these torments we decided that maybe scurvy would be more endurable than fruit flies, and so overboard went the rest of the bananas, along with their little fellow passengers. We felt little sympathy for their fate, right in the middle of the Atlantic; there was no future for them, but at least they left us when the bananas did.

From then on we had idyllic sailing. We had cruised together so much that we were absolutely compatible, and with just the two of us one would always be busy at the helm or sewing a sail or navigating or cooking or resting, so we did not get in each other's way. And we were so close that usually no communication was necessary when a crisis arose. We automatically did what was necessary, perhaps reefing a sail or taking it down, and when the whole job was done we would turn to each other in amazement and realize that no word had been spoken.

For me the night watches were particularly enjoyable. I had brought along a star chart and was able to identify many new constellations we had not seen before, including, of course, the Southern Cross. The air was so clear that very often we would see a light on the horizon, which we would take to be the masthead light on a vessel approaching us. But it was just the planet Venus rising in the east.

With both square sails set the ship steered herself very well when the tiller was lashed, and so it was not necessary to stay at the helm all the time. One could go below and brew up a cup of cocoa or tea, look at the pilot books, and otherwise entertain oneself. We rotated the night watches every night so we each had a turn of inspecting the decks as the dawn broke. And we often found several sizable flying fish that had landed during the night. We found these to make a delicious breakfast.

When we had about reached the halfway mark I happened to glance over the transom one morning and was surprised to see a fish of about a foot in length swimming gamely behind us. He stayed quite close to the stern and was obviously getting a great deal of help from the deadwater under the stern. He continued to stay there day after day, and we decided to name him Percy after someone I knew who had the same quizzical expression on his face. Percy stayed faithfully in our wake for many days, and we wondered when he was able to get a square meal. In watching him one day, while passing some Sargasso weed, we saw him dart out, grab something, and then immediately scoot back under our stern. He did have a rather annoyed expression on his face as if to complain that we might have waited for him while he had his breakfast. From then on whenever we passed a patch of drifting weed we would reach over and grab it up and see what was in it, for many small creatures have adapted to living in this floating weed: small shrimp, pipefish, and a remarkable butterfish with appendages that looked almost like arms, with which it was able to grasp the branches of the weed.

So Percy was thus able to sustain himself, and it was not until we reached our landfall in Antigua that he finally abandoned us, perhaps scorning to enter the shallow water where he no longer belonged. We have yet to find out what species he was, but I have never seen his like before or since. We were grateful to him, for he did provide us with much interest and discussion. Sometimes we would remark on his looks; perhaps he might appear a little peaked one morning and other times much more exuberant. To become anthropomorphic about a fish was merely one way in which we amused ourselves, and then of course there were often dolphins, tropic birds, and even whales, so we never lacked for interest.

While still several days from reaching the West Indies, we began seeing flocks of birds heading southward. This was now mid-October, and we realized that we were witnessing part of the great annual migration from North America to the tropics. These were land birds, and I could identify some as golden plover. They had probably taken their departure from Newfoundland or Nova Scotia and were heading directly on the long flight to South America. And I wondered: could this be the same species that Columbus had sighted on his first exploratory voyage into the unknown? It is quite likely. Like me, Columbus was a naturalist, and had he not been, or had he left the Canaries at any other season, the history of America's discovery might be different. For his crew were becoming fearful of sailing off the edge of the world, and there were mutterings of a mutiny. But those sightings heartened them, and Columbus, knowing that these were land birds, changed course from west to southwest and thus reached the Bahamas, which he would have missed on his original course. Those several hundred more miles to go before making a landfall might well have been the difference between success and failure.

At last, after twenty-eight days, we were due for a landfall on Antigua. That night, for the first time during the entire passage, we had squalls, and in these squalls, coming surprisingly out of the west, we caught scents that were half-forgotten, those of rain-moistened soil and burned vegetation. It was an anxious night; we knew we were near to land, but we wanted to be sure that our chronometer had been maintaining its steady rate, thus giving us true daily noon positions. So as dawn approached we strained our eyes, and at last we could see a faint blur on the skyline that we knew must be land. It was indeed Antigua, and in a very short time we were sailing triumphantly into Saint John's Harbour, sunburned, bearded, and naked, but proud of our achievement. It had been a delightful voyage and we were filled with pride for our ship and for ourselves.

This was 1931, and Antigua was still unknown to the tourists' world. There were, in fact, very few whites on the island, but those who were received us with open arms and very quickly introduced us to the rum swizzle and other Caribbean delights. Their hospitality and friendship were unbounded, especially that of several young ladies who worked in the local government offices and banks. It was hard to get away, but we realized that our meager funds would soon be drastically depleted if we remained. We were told of Tortola in the British Virgin Islands to the westward as an island seldom visited and therefore a good place in which we could settle down to write some articles we had promised to mail back to England.

Before sailing on to Tortola, we stopped at the neighboring island of Barbuda. This is an island that was very seldom visited, since there was no proper harbor and the only anchorage was somewhat exposed and dotted with coral heads. It had a great appeal to us. It abounded with wildlife, including guinea fowl that had been introduced from Africa, but also with many native birds, including a large colony of frigate birds. During the bad old slavery days it had become a kind of stud farm for producing a superior race of slaves. Consequently, all the finest specimens of both male and female were brought over there to breed and produce a higher grade of working slave. The stature of the people of Barbuda is certainly striking, as they are far above the norm.

We had an exciting several days on the island, hunting with some of these people, and it was here that we gained another shipmate. The island abounded with land tortoises, and the Barbudians had trained small dogs, known as turtle hounds, to hunt for these tortoises, turn them on their backs when found, and bark until their owner arrived to retrieve the tortoise for a future meal. There was one skinny brown dog that took our fancy. A gentle little creature, she was half-starved, like most of the island dogs, but nevertheless there was something about her that took our fancy. So when it came time to leave, the owner, who had several other well-trained turtle hounds, was willing to part with her. So Tiger, as she was called, joined our crew. She proved to be a marvelous little sea dog and adapted very quickly to life on board and was a faithful friend for the next few years, going through many vicissitudes with great aplomb.

Approaching the British Virgins from the east, we entered the Sir Francis Drake Channel, which is formed between Tortola and a chain of small islands to the south.

Some of these islands have intriguing names like Dead Man's Chest and Fallen Jerusalem; others are more prosaic, like Peter, Norman, and Round. But they were all waterless and uninhabited except for clouds of seabirds on some, and they serve as perfect satellites for the queen, Tortola, the largest island, with its higher, greener mountains, the central focus of the entire group. Road Town Harbour, on Tortola's south coast, is surrounded by an amphitheater of wooded shoreline. Here we found a pleasant, well-protected anchorage in a beautiful setting.

There were five white families on the island, including one local planter and his wife, a doctor, an administrator, and a minister. They all proved to be extremely friendly and we very soon settled into life ashore, for a small hut was put at our disposal where we had a little more room to write. For the next couple of months we were able to become quite productive.

By this time we were down to our last few shillings and were wondering what our next move should be, when out of the blue appeared two young Americans with a proposal that was close to our own desire. Recently graduated from Yale University, they had come to Puerto Rico and Saint Thomas looking for a sailboat in which they could cruise through the Caribbean Islands. In these days of whole fleets of yachts for charter in the Caribbean, it is hard to believe that they could not find anything available, but this was in 1932. Then, in a chance conversation in a Saint Thomas bar they heard about us, and so they came to Tortola to see if they could persuade us to sail with them up and down the Lesser Antillean chain. Since they were ready to pay the running expenses of the ship, we did not hesitate to agree, and the cruise was on.

With a little imagination, one could easily believe that nature had the sailorman in mind when she created the islands of the Lesser Antilles. She was reserving a part of the world's oceans where the sailing would be idyllic. First, there must be fresh and constant breezes and plenty of warm sunshine. Second, there must be a line of many islands, not too far from one another, just one good day's sail from one to the next one. Third, the chain must run in a roughly north and south direction, so that the trade winds would blow directly across it. Thus, vessels could sail up or down the chain without the need to tack. For about nine months of the year the trades blow, strong and steady, from somewhere betweeen ENE and ESE, but usually from ENE. There are no fogs, few thunder squalls, and never a snowflake. It is only in the months of July, August, and September that the winds become unsteady and are interspersed with calms. Every few years, in one of those erratic months, nature develops a hurricane. Perhaps, as an afterthought, she must not spoil the sailor completely; a hurricane once in a while is just the reminder he needs to maintain a proper respect for her. For the rest of the year, he has conditions all his own way.

John Green and Don Hoggson turned out to be splendid shipmates, and the cruise we had with them was idyllic. In those days, Hilton Hotels were unheard of, and cruise ships had yet to find a ready market for travel-hungry tourists in the Caribbean. It seemed as if we had these lovely islands to ourselves, as we vagabonded through the chain. Each island was different, some British, some French, some Dutch, each with its own ambiance. We swam among the coral reefs, we climbed the forest-clad hills, we made friends with the local people, we marketed for the local fruits and vegetables, and we fished for our dinners. Thus several pleasant months passed, until our two friends had to return to the United States and Geoff and I reluctantly turned north, back to Saint Thomas. Little did I know then how that chance conversation in a Saint Thomas bar was to affect both of our futures.

We returned to Tortola, an island for which we had developed a strong affection, and had again settled down to write when Rev. John Levo came to us with an interesting proposition. He was the owner of a fine coconut plantation at Belmont, at the western end of the island. Several years before, a hurricane had partially destroyed his house and severely damaged the coconut trees. He was wondering if we would be interested in moving out to Belmont for a year, taking charge of the coconut plantation to prevent the pilfering that was going on at the time and also making what profit we could out of the nuts by sailing them to the main market for them, which was on the island of Saint Thomas. This sounded like a fine arrangement; we would have a place to live, with a bay close by where we could keep *Uldra* to use her to sail the nuts down to Saint Thomas every few weeks, thereby acquiring a little income and at the same time helping to improve the plantation itself.

We found Belmont to be an idyllic location, but the living was indeed primitive, since there was only one small corner of the house that still had a roof to it. But here we would at least have shelter. We would have plenty of time for our writing and could also work on freeing the coconut palms of vines and creepers, clearing away brush from around the trees, and thereby discouraging the nearby Tortolans from helping themselves to the ripe nuts as they fell to the ground. There was a water tank in front of the house with a dead rat floating in it.

We fished him out and were careful to boil our drinking water from then on. We made arrangements with the nearby village for our bread to be brought to us every few days and also an occasional haunch of goat meat. Otherwise we had our dinghy with which we could maintain a trap and have fresh fish when we needed it. We made a pen for the large land crabs that were abundant on the island. By feeding them on kitchen scraps for a few days they became succulent and good eating, in spite of their somewhat unhealthy appearance. At the end of the day we could go down to the beach nearby and take a refreshing swim, then go back to the house to light our kerosene lantern and do our reading and writing.

Several months passed by as we settled down to a regular routine, and then we entered the season of Caribbean hurricanes, which generally occur in the months of July, August, and September. This was a period when the erstwhile steady tradewinds become very fitful, with calms and thunderstorms. Sometimes we had heavy rains lasting for several days. We watched the sky and the barometer for signs of trouble, and on the advice of some of the local islanders we also watched the seabirds, for they, we were told, would be heard wailing distressfully before a storm struck. We took it in turns going over the mountains for a social visit in Road Town every few weeks, and this was a relief from the loneliness at Belmont. One weekend during September, Geoff took off over the hills, as it was his turn for Road Town hospitality. As he set off down the trail I laughingly said, "Watch out for Old Man Hurricane on the way."

The next day the sky was overcast and there was a hazy look to windward; then I heard the plaintive calling. A flock of noddy terns was circling aimlessly over the shore, and there was a note in their cries I had not heard before. One of the local Tortolans came over to warn me that he was quite sure that a hurricane was on its way, as he was guided by the calling of the noddies. He warned me that when it came on to blow, I should not stay in the house, but go to a tiny daub-and-wattle shack that had been built by the workmen down in a hollow many years ago when they built the main house.

When I was quite certain that the hurricane was on its way, I gathered up our most precious possessions, our books, notes, photos, and the typewriter, and took them down to the little shack. Back in the house I picked up a lantern, some food, and a bottle of milk, closed the shutters and doors as well as I could, and called Tiger, who followed closely at my heels. We were halfway to the little shack when the first squall hit. The air was filled with sand, leaves, and twigs, then came a solid sheet of rain. When the squall was over, the wind settled down to a steady blast, gradually increasing until it did not seem possible it could get any worse. The voice of the wind rose to a discordant shriek, punctuated by the cracking of limbs and the pattering of pebbles and twigs on the walls of my little shelter. The hours dragged by. I dozed off, then suddenly awoke to realize that there was a new condition outside.

There was no more sound except for the distant moaning of the sea. The night was so black I could not see a thing beyond the rays of the lantern. Outside, the ground was a churned-up mass of mud, leaves, twigs, and fallen trees. There was just this horrifying silence. I was wondering if it was all over when I heard a whisper, a sigh, and a mutter and then the distant roar like an express train coming out of a tunnel. The wind was back; I knew then that the hurricane was not over. I had just been in the center; now the second half was assailing the island. Now the wind was in the southwest. And in the next few minutes it was blowing harder than ever.

It was not until morning that I thought I could detect a change in its tempo; there was no longer that terrible screech, and there was no more pattering of pebbles against the walls. I was then sure the hurricane was leaving us to pass on to other islands. The sunrise was one of the most glorious I have ever seen. The whole sky was filled with pink in all its delicate shades from the deep rose of a conch shell to the faint blush of apple blossom. Around me the trees were a twisted mass of splintered limbs.

When I returned to the house I found the contents all in turmoil. In spite of my having fastened everything down, one of the windows had burst in and the whole interior was spattered with rain, leaves, and sand. Everything had been picked up and whirled around in a mad dance. I was in despair. I sat down on the rocks and bowed my head in my hands, when a wet nose was pushed lightly against my arm. Tiger was doing her best to cheer me up, reminding me I still had her. "Thank God for that," I said with as much cheerfulness as I could muster.

Later in the day, Geoff came back as fast as he could, hoping that I was safe. He was able to cheer me up by telling me that *Uldra* was also safe. She had been blown up on a sandbank and had stayed there until it was all over. He had gotten some help in floating her again, and she was now safe at her anchorage. It took us a long time before we were back to normal. But we finally got the plantation more or less in order again.

We had been there for about eight months when Geoff became violently ill, and I had no idea what his problem was. He had a high fever, and fortunately I fed him with the only food that was safe for him, and that was mashed bananas. As it developed later, when the island launch was able to round the coast into Belmont Bay and take him back to the hospital in Road Town, he had typhoid fever and would need several months of convalescence in Road Town before he could become fully active.

I stayed on and completed the year at the plantation. It was a lonely existence, and I often found myself talking to Tiger, as if she understood. I was more than ever thankful for her companionship, and she always stuck close to my heels. In spite of the storm, the damage to the coconut trees was minimal. Most of the ripe nuts had been blown down and needed to be gathered into sacks. I made arrangements with one of the Tortola sloops to ship them to the Saint Thomas market. I thus ended my brief career as a coconut farmer.

3

A Change of Course

By the end of the year we had agreed upon with Rev. John Levo, Geoff was almost recovered and we were thinking of moving on when our lives were changed by the arrival of the American yacht *Pinta*, a forty-seven-foot Alden-designed schooner. Who should be on board but our former shipmate John Green, who had cruised with us in the Lesser Antilles over a year ago? The rest of the crew had left except for one paid hand, and they needed help in sailing *Pinta* to New York, since this was March, a season of uncertain weather. Could Geoff and I be available? At that time we had absolutely no plan to visit that part of the world. The South Seas were beckoning us much more emphatically than the Americas. It sounded tempting, however, since we might be able to find work up there to add to our small funds and thus enable us to extend the cruise farther into the South Pacific. Moreover, the vessel's owner would pay our passage back to Tortola. So we signed on. John Green was in command; with him was a large amiable Danish sailor named Emil. Immediately, when Emil saw Tiger, he became a big, soft, simpering, jellylike mass of love. To him Tiger was irresistible; he fussed over her at every conceivable moment.

Before we took off, of course, we had to do something about *Uldra*. Fortunately, at the entrance to Road Town Harbour there was an extensive mangrove swamp penetrated by several shallow creeks. This made a perfect shelter for our little vessel, which we hated to leave. But we convinced ourselves that it would be only a very brief separation. We knew she could come to no harm in such a well-protected mooring, with the dense mangroves serving as perfect protection against high winds and seas. So we took off, little realizing what was in store for us, but nevertheless hoping that this would eventually help us get closer to the South Pacific, even though we were heading in precisely the wrong direction to our ultimate objective.

We sailed up through the Bahamas and soon realized the admirable sailing qualities of this lovely vessel. She was much livelier than *Uldra*; it was like comparing a greyhound to a good, honest retriever. We headed up for the entrance to Chesapeake Bay, but as we drew nearer to the coast of North Carolina the weather turned very bad. Geoff and I had completed our watch and we were expecting to be called soon to put the ship about, since we were on the starboard tack and this was bringing us closer to the coast. Perhaps John was unaware that there was a strong set-in shore and that we should have come about before we did. It must have been near midnight, with a strong northeast wind, when we struck the outer bar. *Pinta* was heeled over at a steep angle, and sheets of water drenched us as we struggled to take down the sails.

At first John thought we were on some offlying shoal and the situation looked grim, but upon shining a flashlight over on the port side we could see sand and above the sandy beach some dunes covered in grass, so we knew we were on the mainland. Thus, staggering through the surf, I first stepped foot on what was to become my homeland, in a howling gale, at midnight, on the lonely coast of Cape Hatteras. The seas forced *Pinta* onto the shore, and the pounding soon ceased. We brought ashore what valuables we could and hoped for the best.

Soon the Coast Guard appeared, fine men who were accustomed to the many wrecks occurring on that part of the shore, and they were in no way discouraging about the possibilities of getting the ship off. Sure enough, the following day the winds swung around, a Coast Guard vessel arrived offshore, they ran a cable ashore and passed it around the hull, and at high tide off she came. Thus we continued our voyage and got her up to Norfolk. She was somewhat scarred but otherwise undamaged. Of course, everything inside was a soggy mess, but at least she had survived, as *Pinta* has survived many other near disasters in her long, charmed life.

So there we were in a new country, but far from homeless. Hospitality reached out to us on every side. We were driven up to Long Island, where past friends invited us to stay with them, and I quickly found a job running a motorboat on Long Island Sound for an elderly lady. It was not very exciting, but it was a paying job, and it did enable me to become familiar with the many fine harbors on the sound and meet many of the local yachtsmen.

It was then that another maritime disaster occurred: Geoff fell in love. This looked like the end of a partnership that had endured many vicissitudes and many rewards. He was deeply enamored of Nickie, and there was little that could be done about it, of course. They decided to return to *Uldra*, but in the meantime, I found other opportunities in the States and so agreed to rejoin them later. With the summer at an end, my job on Long Island Sound also ended, and I was considering heading back to the Caribbean when another offer arose that would be taking me ever farther from that ultimate objective, the South Pacific.

Carl Weagant, a yachtsman who had already sailed from New York to the Mediterranean in the sloop *Carlsark*, had become intrigued by the story of a treasure waiting to be recovered on the Silver Shoals north of the island of Hispaniola. A fleet of galleons bearing much treasure destined for the Mother Church in Spain set out from the port now known as Puerto Plata on the north coast of Santo Domingo in the month of September, the worst month for hurricanes in the Caribbean. The admiral, in spite of warnings of bad weather, claimed that God would protect his fleet, since they were bearing treasure for the church. Shortly after the fleet sailed they were caught by a hurricane, and several of the vessels were lost on the coral reefs forming that treacherous area known as Silver Shoals.

Many years after these wrecks a venturesome New Englander, William Phipps, became intrigued with the possibility of retrieving some of that treasure and, obtaining finances from the royal court in Britain, formed an expedition. Using Carib Indian divers, they searched the reefs under the most difficult conditions, and they were about to abandon the project when a diver brought up a sea fan with an ingot of silver attached to it. From then on, the divers began recovering more and more silver bars and other treasure from one of the wrecks that had broken up, with its cargo scattered over the floor of the sea, in about forty feet of water. Phipps returned to England in triumph and was eventually knighted and appointed as the first governor of the new colony of Massachusetts. There were no other accounts of riches having been recovered from these wrecks, and a researcher had studied records of the trial in Spain of the admiral who was responsible for losing so much of the treasure, valued at many millions of dollars. It was obvious that a great deal more was scattered on the reefs, awaiting salvage by anyone willing to face the difficulties of working in such an exposed, dangerous area.

Carl had located in Newfoundland a seventy-two-foot schooner named *Marit* that would be suitable for a small expedition to try to recover some of the treasure. By this time it was late in the year, and it was a race against time to bring the schooner down to New York before she became iced in for the winter. I was asked to join this exciting venture. There were five of us; we were driven by Carl's mother to Cape Breton Island, and from there we took the ferry across Cabot Straits, and thence by train to Corner Brook in the Bay of Islands, on the west coast of Newfoundland. I certainly had splendid shipmates: Coulton Waugh, with whom I had sailed on the *Pinta*, a fine marine artist and excellent company; Slade Dale, another experienced cruising man; Rufus Smith, well known in small-boat circles; and Carl himself.

We reached the schooner just in time; a skim of ice was already forming around her hull, and as soon as we got aboard we raised the two anchors and got the auxiliary engine going and moved across the bay to the small town of Corner Brook, where we could take on supplies. These were extremely limited and consisted mostly of frozen herring. We did find a few cans in the local store, but that was about all. We realized that we had to get away soon, as it was already late November, when the upper end of the bay freezes over for the winter. We set sail and headed down the Humber Arm as it began to snow and entered the Gulf of Saint Lawrence, by which time the wind had shifted around to the northwest. We realized we must get as much of an offing from that rock-bound coast as possible. We had reefed down the mainsail and had the storm jib set on the bowsprit, so *Marit* was all snugged down.

It was a very lively night, especially since my four shipmates became seasick. It was deathly cold and the spray that came on board was forming a sheathing of ice. However, we had received several very valuable pieces of advice before we sailed from Corner Brook: one was to install in the main cabin a round-belly stove, which became affectionately known as Red-Hot Jenny. Also, we were given, by one of the local fishermen, some icing mallets. Made out of short sections of birch log, with long handles, they were of vital importance in freeing the masses of ice that form on decks and rigging in these northern latitudes. We were also warned to take along a sack of rock salt to put in the deck pump to prevent it from freezing. All this advice was accepted gratefully and undoubtedly contributed to our being able to complete this difficult passage successfully.

By next morning the weather side of the ship and the decks were thickly clad in ice. All the halyards were frozen into iron bars and could not possibly run through the blocks; handling sails was out of the question. With the weight of all this ice, the ship was laboring awkwardly, and we knew we must get busy with the icing mallets. But first we took a bucketful of ashes from Red-Hot Jenny's belly and sprinkled them on the decks to give us a better footing. It was hard, dangerous work, and it says much for the fortitude of my seasick shipmates that they kept at the job until the ship's motion became more bouyant and lively. Fortunately, the wind held constant in the northwest, and by the following day we sighted the rugged cliffs of Cape North, on Cape Breton Island, up to windward.

Soon we were out in the Atlantic, heading for the warmer waters of the Gulf Stream, where we would be able to rid ourselves of the last of our icy burden. Once east of Sable Island we began to notice the difference, as chunks of ice fell from the rigging and slithered around the decks until disintegrating through the scuppers. The wind moderated and we could at length set all sail and lay a course for the Cape Cod Canal.

The 1,207-mile passage to New York took nine days and eighteen hours, but by the time we sailed up Long Island Sound we were seasoned Arctic sailors. The vessel must have made a fine sight as we came tearing through the Arctic smoke into Port Washington in the early morning, with our hull glistening with ice and all sails set. We hated to have to get rid of our icy decorations, for the main boom was festooned with many dozens of clinging icicles and the windward side of the hull was completely sheathed in a coat of ice. And so we came to anchor after a thrilling trip, with one can of beef and two of salmon our only remaining supplies.

The expedition to Silver Shoals, when we had finally equipped the vessel for her salvage work, did not involve us in any particularly bad weather, but we were burdened by a large compressor and a pair of dories for workboats. We had two experienced ex–navy divers on board, and all we had to do was to find the wreck, or so we thought. We put in at Puerto Plata, and there were Geoff and Nickie and the *Uldra* to meet us, so we had a great reunion. They waited until our attempted salvage was to come to an end.

Silver Shoals is a terrible place; on the chart it is a large area bounded by a dotted line, enclosing the simple words: "numerous shoals and reefs in this area." It has never been properly charted and presumably never will be; it is just a place to be avoided whenever possible. Approaching it, one sees the breakers rising all around the horizon, and it is only safe to move in this area when the sun is high and one can see clearly, from the masthead, the many coral reefs scattered in all directions. To anchor there requires a constant watch, because the chain becomes caught in the coral and she surges in the ever-present swells. So one must always be alert to the possibility of dragging anchor or parting the chain. The rolling and pitching is continuous, so life on board is very uncomfortable.

We started out by surveying with the two dories for the possibility of wrecks, and in three days we located several of them. But it was on the fourth day, when we saw cannons of the period in which we were interested scattered on the bottom, that we knew we had located one of the galleons we were looking for. We then began diving and realized how inadequate our equipment was for the work in hand. The sand had obviously buried most of the hull, and surely what treasure there was had been in that part of the vessel. We needed some type of elaborate sand sucker, which we did not have. We found cannons, cannonballs, and masses of clay pipes, pike heads, and other weapons, but it was obvious that we would be unable to uncover any treasure with our equipment. So after several weeks of work and disappointment we gave up and headed back to Puerto Plata, where I rejoined *Uldra* and headed northward. It had been for me an interesting experience, and since I was not one of the investors who had financed the expedition I was not as disappointed as the others were.

We sailed *Uldra* north through the Bahamas, then up the coast and eventually into New York Harbor. It was a Sunday when we came sailing into the lower bay.

We flew our British Red Ensign, and we were obviously a foreign vessel.

The Customs and Immigration vessel, many times our size, approached us, and some very merry officials, who had obviously been enjoying a quiet Sunday, came close to us and yelled across, "Where are you from?"

"The Bahamas," we said.

"Got any parrots or orchids on board?"

We shook our heads. A few more questions, a few bottles waved in our direction, some friendly smiles, and one of these officials waved his arms, pointed up the harbor, and said, "Go ahead, kids; the city is yours," and we sailed on with a cheer.

Before we set sail from England Geoff and I had made an agreement, whereby, should one of us back out of the partnership for any reason, the other partner would take over that partner's share of the ship. Since by this time Geoff and Nickie had decided to return to England and that Geoff should resume his business in London, I was then in possession of *Uldra*, but minus one of the finest shipmates I have ever had. I was extremely wary of signing up another shipmate without being certain of his compatibility in every aspect of sharing a twenty-nine-foot boat for months and possibly years on end.

In the meantime I was presented with another very pleasant opportunity, not only to earn some money, but to have a job that appealed to me immensely, and that was to become a sailing instructor at the American Yacht Club, in Rye, New York. I have always enjoyed young people, and teaching them to sail, and being able to live on my own boat in the meantime, was the most delightful way to spend the summer while I was planning my future.

So Tiger and I had a job. For instruction we sailed a small sloop called the *Wee Scot*. There were many eager young boys and girls to teach, the yacht club was nearby, and all the friendly yachtsmen there came to know me well, and so summer passed in this very pleasant fashion.

In 1934 the women's sailing championships were being held at the American Yacht Club. It was one of my responsibilities to help out, as much as possible, with the committee work involved in this weeklong series of races. Little did I realize then how this was to affect my future. The Atlantic class was being used for the races. The Atlantic is a lively boat and quite fast. Although I always had an eye out for attractive women, most of the females I had checked out so far at these races did not seem too appealing to me. They were rather inclined to be the husky, muscular, mannish type, and since I had been somewhat starved for femininity, I was hoping for something in the line of 100 percent female. The races proceeded in due course, and as happens so many times on Long Island Sound during the summer, the wind died before one of the races was over. The boats were becalmed with sails hanging limply in the middle of the Sound, far from the finish line, with little hope of the usual evening "shotgun" breeze, as it has come to be known locally.

So two of us were sent out in the committee boat to tow the boats in. We picked up a long train of them and were towing them in, while I watched to see that everything was in good order as my shipmate was at the helm. Suddenly from the fourth boat in the line I saw a female figure describe an arc in the air and land in the water with a splash. I yelled to the helmsman to cut the engine, under the impression that someone had fainted or had some kind of seizure. Without hesitation I jumped overboard and swam over. Just then a blond head bobbed up and I said, "Are you all right?" and she said, "Yes, I'm fine. How are you?" We got her aboard and she explained what had happened. The towline had jumped out of the towing chock and the boat was yawing in an unpleasant manner, so she went forward to try to get the towline back into the chock, when it flipped across the deck, caught her ankle, and tossed her overboard.

She was Betty Wellington, a student at Bennington College in Vermont and a resident of Long Island and New York City, a member of the Great South Bay racing team, and a most attractive young lady. I came to know more of her during the rest of the race week, and she gave me her address in New York. Perhaps she was intrigued by the fact that I had come from far away and was living a somewhat unusual life. By a remarkable coincidence when she returned to Bennington in the fall she discovered that her roommate was the daughter of the commodore of the American Yacht Club, who had expressed an interest in my seagoing travels. So for the next three years I wrote to him periodically describing my adventures. In this way, Betty was able to keep up with my whereabouts, and so, when I returned to the States in late 1937, she contacted me when I was invited to give a lecture at the American Yacht Club recounting my cruising experiences. There, a chance meeting in the waters of mid–Long Island Sound had resulted in the most significant development in my life. But all that came three years later.

4

Heading for the South Seas

Again, at the end of the summer, this temporary job of sailing instruction came to an end, and I was hesitant to pick up an unknown to accompany me to the Pacific. Then I received an invitation that carried great appeal to me. Two young Americans, Bruce and Sheridan Fahnestock, had recently acquired a forty-five-foot schooner and were planning a voyage to the South Pacific. They had been in contact with some people at the American Museum of Natural History and had some requests to collect certain materials for the habitat exhibits in the planning stage at the museum. Neither Bruce nor Sheridan had any experience in celestial navigation. They had heard of me and had contacted me at the American Yacht Club and asked me if I could sail over to Port Washington to see them. This I did, and I was soon on board their sturdy schooner, named *Director*. She had once been the Portland, Maine, pilot schooner and was a stout vessel with obviously many sea-kindly attributes.

The two Fahnestock brothers, Bruce and Sheridan, impressed me greatly at first. They seemed enthusiastic, outgoing, and warm, and I, like so many others, was quickly under their spell. They told me they had arrangements for collecting specimens for the museum, that my artistic interests would enable me to make a big contribution in sketching wildlife in more remote areas, and that my navigational abilities would be extremely helpful. All of these early promises made me feel that I was on the right ship with the right people. Little did I realize some of the disillusionment that would follow.

Soon after I came aboard, I heard a deep voice alongside as a launch came out from shore. A burly man in his fifties climbed aboard and began patting the ship approvingly, talking nonstop, introducing himself as Dick Nugent, who had once sailed on this little vessel when she was a pilot schooner off the Maine coast. He was obviously very much in love with the ship and deeply interested in the cruise on which she was bound. He was one of these outgoing people who go overboard in their enthusiasms, and he quickly made us realize that he would be of great help to us. He was firmly convinced that natives in the South Seas would love shiny, gaudy buttons and buckles. On the basis of this, he had a friend print up some stationery with the heading "R. S. Nugent Button Company," along with his address. He then found names of button and buckle companies all over the United States and sent out letters to them, mentioning his business in the button world and requesting samples of their wares. Pretty soon samples arrived in unbounded quantities, resulting in a large chest full of brilliant decorations of all kinds, shapes, colors, and degrees of gaudiness. These we found eventually to be valuable trade goods.

This was only one of the ways in which Dick Nugent managed to manifest his enthusiasm in our cruise. He, as I, was intrigued thoroughly by the plans that were expounded about the coming adventure. The rest of the year, 1934, was devoted to preparing the ship, now bearing the impressive title of Fahnestock South Sea Expedition. I never could quite discover what was the purpose of the expedition, beyond the consumption of large quantities of alcoholic refreshment in the various ports that we visited.

I, however, was not the only naturalist on board. We were joined by two young naturalists from Oklahoma: Hugh Davis, the curator of the Tulsa (Oklahoma) Zoo, who had distinguished himself as an assistant to the Martin Johnson expeditions in Africa, and a young assistant, Wilson Glass. It was regrettable that these two fine people only remained with us as far as Panama. They had had enough by that time.

Before we sailed, I had the responsibility of ensuring *Uldra*'s future welfare. Some friends in the Cruising Club of America were more than pleased to take care of her and use her until Geoff decided how to dispose of her, since I notified him that she was now in his hands. Subsequently, he and Nickie did return to the United States and sailed *Uldra* back to the Virgin Islands. During World War II, Geoff worked at the U.S. submarine base in Saint Thomas; but following the war, when I tried to get in touch with him, I learned to my great sorrow that he had died from some tropical disease. *Uldra*, which had been lying at anchor in the harbor, was caught in a hurricane, swept out to sea, and broke up on a reef. So I never saw that beloved little ship again, but I will always remember her with the strongest affection.

We set out appropriately, on the first of January 1935, and luckily we had good but strong northwest winds to carry us across the Gulf Stream into tropical waters. We made a nonstop passage all the way to the Panama Canal. We anticipated a quick transit to the canal, using, of course, the diesel engine. Bruce Fahnestock was the engineer, and it soon developed that the engine was more than he could cope with. Although we managed to get through the first set of locks into Gatun Lake, the engine then broke down completely and we were obliged to actually sail through the lake. The pilot was delighted to be sailing, but obviously we could not carry on through the other series of locks until the engine was operating. So we had the pleasant experience of spending two weeks in Gatun Lake itself. For us three naturalists this was a delight.

In the lake are many small wooded islands; they were the tops of hills before the land was flooded as part of the canal system. Much wildlife has concentrated on these islands, and with the rowboat we spent many exciting days photographing, sketching, and studying birds, mammals, and reptiles that were new to us. I caught a three-foot boa constrictor there; he was amenable to handling, and so I adopted him as a pet, naming him Egbert and keeping him in a box on the cabin top. There will be more about him later.

The two brothers spent most of their time in the local bars, and it was an odd phenomenon that the higher their consumption of alcohol, the more belligerent they became. This involved getting into fights with innocent barflies and being quite cantankerous when they returned on board. It quickly became clear that the cruise ahead of us was not going to be one constant source of pleasure, and the two Oklahomans could see that the so-called expedition was not to be anything with which they wanted to be associated. Since I had already invested all my savings in the cruise, I realized that I must stick it out and find what pleasure I could in spite of the drawbacks. Of course, the cruise was not all bad; when we were at sea things went fairly well and when we were in a port where bars were nonexistent this also could be quite pleasurable. But I soon realized to my disappointment that the "expedition" was a complete sham.

Although we lost the two Oklahomans, we did take on another shipmate, of an entirely different character.

It happened this way: *Seth Parker*, a large four-masted American schooner, while cruising through the Polynesian islands had picked up a young Marquesan sailor as a deckhand. Later the vessel was in difficulties while being battered by a hurricane off the Samoan islands. She sent out an SOS, and the nearest ship to answer her call was the HMS *Australia*, heading for Panama after a state visit to Australia. She took off most of the personnel on the schooner, leaving a handful on board to await the arrival of a rescue tug. The *Australia* continued on her way to Panama and disembarked all the castaways there. All but one were then able to make their way back to the United States. That one who remained was the young Marquesan sailor. The Panamanian authorities did not know what to do with him, so they locked him up in a quarantine station. Unable to communicate in his broken French, the bewildered lad could not understand his predicament. His carefree life as a sailor seemed at an end. In desperation, he escaped by climbing the fence and wandered the streets of Panama City until picked up by the police and retuned to his prison. He began refusing the food they offered him; he was like a wild bird that had been trapped and caged, longing for freedom. It was about then, with the engine again operating, that we made our transit through the canal and anchored off Balboa to take on supplies, and the authorities realized that we could be the answer to their problem. We were heading for the islands; would we sign him on? One look at him, and our hearts opened to him.

Tehate Teiheikeihonotoua Fiu, for that was his Marquesan name, was a handsome lad, with coal black hair, skin the color of mahogany, and gleaming white teeth. When I explained to him in my fractured French that we were going to take him along on a schooner, his sad expression disappeared in a happy grin. Once on board, he became a changed person, laughing and whooping with joy, clambering up the mast, and generally expressing his exuberance to be free again. We found him to be a great addition to the crew and were sorry when he eventually left us in Tahiti.

When we sailed from Balboa and entered the great Pacific Ocean for the first time, our first islands were the Perlas archipelago, a group embodying in minature the lush jungles of Central America. As their name indicates, they were once an important source of pearls, probably some of the first to be seen by Europeans. The Spanish settlers found that the Indians, unaware of the value of pearls, had amassed great quantities of them while diving for shellfish and were willing to barter them in return for relatively worthless trinkets. There is no longer much pearl diving now, but on Isla del Rey the local people did have a few that could be traded for salt, rice, fish hooks, and tobacco.

San José, another island in the group, was uninhabited, due, we were told, to the appearance at night of the headless ghost of a Spaniard walking up and down the beach, uttering mournful cries. We anchored in a small, forest-lined bay at the southernmost end of the island. Due to the heat, I rolled up in a blanket and slept on deck, to be awakened at dawn by a discordant screech. For a moment I thought of the ghost, but it was just a pair of parrots on an *erythrina* tree limb almost directly overhead.

Since wildlife was abundant, Bruce went ashore to shoot birds and the rabbitlike agoutis. He was soon successful, but we were all upset by the bloodied bodies of green and red parrots, just like the ones seen in cages and doted on by elderly maiden ladies. But one victim was still alive, only slightly wounded in one wing, and we felt sorry for him and decided to make amends by caring for him and taming him. At first he bit and scratched, but within a week he was so tame we gave him the freedom of the ship. He adapted to shipboard life and became extremely affectionate. His favorite perch was a human shoulder, where he sat quietly, occasionally nibbling gently at the nearest earlobe. Remarkably, he learned, all on his own initiative, to become "shoulder-broken." When he became restless and shuffled his feet, this was his signal for the need to defecate. He would step onto the held-up finger and was then held overside, where he could drop his load. Then, it was back to the shoulder, with a low croon of contentment.

We named him José and made much of him. He seemed to love shipboard life; there were plenty of ropes to climb, boobies to curse at, and woodwork to chew. Even if he was high in the rigging, a call would bring him climbing down as fast as beak and feet would carry him. He became so much a part of the ship's complement, we hated to turn him over to a kindly couple two years later when we reached Kowloon. But we could no longer care for him properly when we were leaving our ship.

We left the Perlas Islands and started out across the Gulf of Panama to the Galápagos Islands. These waters are notorious for their calms, but we were in luck. We had a steady northwest breeze, not very strong, but enough to carry us along at a steady pace, and we made our landfall on Tower Island at the northeast end of the Galápagos, after a seven-day passage, probably some sort of a record for a slow-moving schooner.

As we neared the island, fish were jumping all around us, and we paid out a trolling line with a shiny spoon bait. We had a victim right away, not a fish but a booby. The hook was caught in the skin at the base of the bird's bill, and by the time we hauled him in he was half-drowned. No sooner had we paid out the line again than we had hooked another bird. So we had to give up fishing for a while, but we had more than enough to satisfy us later.

Tower is a beautiful island. It is a sunken crater, and we were able to anchor inside the caldera, near a beach populated by California sea lions, Sally Lightfoot crabs, boobies, frigate birds, marine iguanas, and many other wonderful creatures. To go ashore in such a place was a delight; there was wildlife all around us, and like all the wildlife in the Galápagos, it was quite fearless. This is a peculiarity of several other places in the world that I have come to know quite well, such as the Falkland Islands and Antarctica. These three areas have this in common, that man has only recently intruded there. Thus the birds and animals have not developed an instinctive fear of man and do not regard him as a potential enemy. It is, therefore, a moving experience to be able to come up close to these creatures without them showing any apprehension.

We spent several days on Tower Island and then moved on to several of the other uninhabited ones, before we decided we might as well make it official and check in at one of the few inhabited islands. San Cristobal was then the seat of government for the entire Galápagos. It was also a penal settlement for Ecuadorean convicts. We sailed into the bay, and soon a cloud of dust announced the arrival of a government official, the local *teniente* in charge of the convicts. He had seen our vessel and came on his horse down from the hills. We went ashore in our dinghy and rowed him out. There was a fair swell, and the ship was rolling quite badly. We gave him rum and a can of chili con carne, but pretty soon he began looking green and after he had made a hasty check of our papers he dashed to the side with the usual results. It was then a matter of getting him ashore as quickly as possible, when we were free to roam the rest of the island group.

The Galápagos are also known as *Las Islas Encantadas* (the Enchanted Isles) and by some cynics as the Ash Heap of the Pacific. Until the beginning of large-scale tourism in the 1960s, they were visited mainly by the whalers who stopped there to lay in supplies of fresh meat in the form of the giant land tortoises that once abounded there. The men would land in pairs, carrying one of the long sweeps from the whaleboats. Upon finding a tortoise, it was slung on the oar and carried back to the ship on the men's shoulders. The unfortunate reptiles were then stacked alive on their backs in the hold until ready to be butchered, sometimes many months later. There is an account of a tortoise being found, still living, behind some barrels of whale oil two years after it was taken from its island home.

People without an appreciation for the great beauty and diversity of the wildlife in these islands can readily develop a dislike for them. After all, they are largely just heaps of volcanic lava. Fresh water is very scarce, and at lower levels the vegetation consists mostly of thorny scrub, cactus, and a scattering of other desert plants. But to anyone with a love for the natural world, these islands are as exciting and fascinating an area as anywhere else on earth, with both the islands themselves and their surrounding waters teeming with life on a truly lavish scale.

In those days it was indeed a paradise. There were no restrictions on where one went. We could hunt for goats, we could catch crayfish, we could fish, and the problem in fishing was to get the bait down below the little fish near the surface to the big groupers down below. As we caught the fish we decapitated them, split them open, scored them with a knife, and then rubbed them in rock salt, which we had brought with us from Panama. We laid the fish in the sun and they dried very quickly and thus later in the cruise we had a plentiful supply of protein.

The frigate birds were nesting in the low bushes on some of the islands, and when the males have inflated their huge bright red throat pouches to woo the females, a colony seen at a distance looks like an orchard of some large tropical fruit.

One of the world's most beautiful seabirds is the swallow-tailed gull, endemic to the Galápagos. They were nesting here and feeding their chicks. This gull is peculiar in that it does most of its fishing at night. The tip of its bill is white, and this is the triggering mechanism whereby when the gull chick begs, the white of the bill shows up better in the darkness. The chick reaches for it, and the parent disgorges the food.

In addition to the abundant Galápagos seabirds, there were land birds of many species, all quite fearless. The beautiful little Galápagos dove and the brilliant vermilion flycatcher were very plentiful. In several of the shallow lagoons flocks of bright pink flamingos gave a startling contrast to the blue water. And then there were the Darwin's finches, thirteen different species altogether, dingy little birds but most fascinating of all, because of their remarkably varied bills that enabled them to adapt to the type of food resource on which they subsisted.

We visited several other islands in the group before we came to Floreana. We had heard some gossip in Panama about the strange goings on in this island and the troubles among a few German settlers. There was talk of the mad baroness, who had two lovers who quarreled over her, while she took a sadistic delight in watching them fight. By the time we reached Floreana the baroness and one lover, Philipsohn, had mysteriously disappeared; the other lover, Lorenz, was found dead on the waterless island of Marchena, with a bullet hole in his belly. In the meantime, another German settler, Friedrich Ritter, had died under mysterious circumstances, and his girlfriend, Dora, had left the islands.

The only seemingly sensible family there was the Wittmers. We had a very strange encounter with them. We had received directions in Panama on how to find them, and there was a trail leading up from Post Office Bay, where the famous barrel stood for the receipt and pickup of mail from ingoing and outgoing ships. We followed the trail through arid, typically lowland Galápagos scenery, consisting of lava rock and thorn trees, with a generally dried-up look rather like the African veldt. Eventually we came uphill to more fertile land with green vegetation, then to some bananas and other crops and then to an open space. And there was a peculiar sight. In the middle of the clearing was a naked youth, beautifully formed, probably in his early teens. Beside him was a donkey, and the youth had his arms around the donkey's neck and was whispering into the animal's ear. We stood spellbound for a few moments, wondering if we had come across a performance of *A Midsummer Night's Dream*. As we approached the youth, he heard our footsteps, and he turned around and in German said, "You would like to see my father." He showed absolutely no surprise but led us to the home of the Wittmers.

We were greeted by Herr Wittmer himself, a friendly German in his early forties. His wife was there also. It appeared that the son was retarded, which was obvious to us, but quite harmless. We were received hospitably and found that this resourceful family had everything they needed. They had a bamboo-pipe plumbing installation leading from a small spring, and they appeared to have all the comforts of home, including a hive of bees for honey, many vegetables, and a large hunting dog. With the presence of wild cattle, goats, and pigs on the island there was always plenty of food. Wittmer had many books; he was a well-educated man and spoke some English. He explained that following World War I he had become disgusted with conditions in Germany, and with a son who was incapable of taking care of himself a move to the Galápagos seemed the natural thing to do. We often wondered whether the Wittmers had any hand in the odd incidents affecting other settlers on the island. Years later we heard plenty of gossip that would implicate Mrs. Wittmer. But, be that as it may, there was never any irrefutable evidence connecting her with the odd disappearances of those very unpleasant neighbors.

While on Floreana, Tehate, our Marquesan sailor, was able to prove his worth in a very practical manner. Herr Wittmer had shot a wild pig, which he brought on the back of his donkey to our landing at Post Office Bay. He was planning to roast it on a spit, but Tehate would hear nothing of that idea. He insisted on our letting him take charge and cook the animal in the Polynesian way. First he dug a shallow pit, and in it he started a wood fire. When this had burned down to glowing embers, he piled on the rounded lava rocks from the beach. When they had absorbed sufficient heat, the haunches of pork, carefully wrapped in banana leaves, were added, together with fresh-caught langoustes, rockfish, yams, and roasting bananas, all wrapped in leaves. The food was then covered with the ship's canvas awning, on which sand was generously piled to a depth of several inches. Tehate periodically tested the progress of the hidden food by placing his hand on the sand to tell the temperature. After a couple of hours he indicated that the feast was ready, and the covering was removed. Delicious odors then assailed our nostrils, and we enjoyed a perfectly cooked, memorable feast. Wittmer, somewhat skeptical at first, was so impressed with the results, where none of the juices were lost, that he decided in the future all his meat would be cooked in a *himaa*, or Polynesian oven.

We spent two and a half months in these splendid islands, visiting most of them and doing plenty of fishing and hunting, surprising ourselves by finding penguins, sea lions, fur seals, and albatrosses here, which one usually associates with Antarctic conditions. Oddly enough, the equator runs right through the Galápagos archipelago. It is the Humboldt Current that keeps the islands relatively cool, and since it is rich in nutrients that it carries from the south, the Galápagos are extraordinarily rich in all manner of marine life.

In the early and midseventies I returned as a leader of Audubon groups to these wonderful islands and found many striking changes. With over twenty thousand visitors a year, change was inevitable. Now, only vessels registered in Ecuador are permitted to cruise through the archipelago, and all visitors are herded into small groups led by trained, experienced guides and kept strictly on marked trails. This last requirement is absolutely necessary, or the wildlife would suffer from too much human disturbance. The government of Ecuador is benefitting greatly from this enormous influx of tourists, and it must be credited with doing its best to preserve the unique ecological values of the islands. But we must hope that a realistic limit will be set on the volume of visitors, for in spite of the best intentions, there are already signs of wear and tear that cannot be eradicated. I am thankful that I was one of the privileged few to see the Galápagos as they were before so much of the rest of the world decided to see them, too. Those ten weeks I spent there in 1935 will not be forgotten; they can never be repeated.

5

Islands of Romance

We left the enchanting Galápagos with some regret but were naturally eager to reach the more luxuriant islands of the glamorous South Seas, with their coral-bound lagoons, groves of coconut palms, and grass-skirted maidens. We started out with a fresh northeasterly breeze, but it soon died, making us realize that we were in the notorious doldrums, where calms and fickle breezes prevail, before sailing vessels can pick up the southeast trade winds south of the equator. So for the next ten days we attempted to make every mile of southing we could, instead of laying a more southwesterly course for the Marquesas. This involved a good deal of sail trimming to take advantage of every slight puff, but at length our efforts were rewarded.

A slight wind came out of the east-southeast, it freshened, the sails filled well, and we were at last on our way, reeling off well over 120 miles a day. Dolphins frolicked around our bow, flying fish scattered like frightened quail, and we often saw whales, mostly sperm. When my sights put us about ninety miles from Hiva-Oa, the first of the Marquesas, Tehate climbed the mainmast and said it was there, right over the bow. I could see no land, and surely we were too far away for the island to be visible. But when he descended he pointed with his brown arm, and then I saw what he meant—a distant pile of rounded clouds. Under them I knew there must be mountains—the Marquesas—thirty-two days out from the Galápagos, the South Seas at last!

We reached Nuku Hiva in the Marquesas Islands at the time of Bastille Day, July 14. Since these islands are French, there were great celebrations in the tiny settlement at the head of Tai-o-hae Bay. To our surprise, we found that this was another penal settlement. Criminals from Tahiti were sent to Tai-o-hae. They lived in what was known as a jail, but it was wide open, and the so-called prisoners were free to come and go as they pleased. In fact, to celebrate Bastille Day, they had rigged up a still inside the jail and were having a royal party, to which we were invited. We drank some extremely evil-tasting liquor, which was more than a little powerful. As long as the prisoners went to bed in the jail at night, they were free to come and go as they pleased. This seemed about as easy a way to atone for one's crimes as any we had ever come across.

While in Tai-o-hae Bay we were delighted by the arrival of a fine 130-foot schooner, the *Radio*, owned by Morgan Adams, of San Francisco. She was on her way back to California after visiting Tahiti and Mooréa but had stopped at the Marquesas to stock up on beef, having heard of the many wild cattle on the island.

We joined them on the hunt, taking along several Marquesans to act as guides and porters. *Radio* anchored in Marquisienne Bay, at the western end of the island, and we climbed up the wooded hills to a semiopen plateau. In the distance a herd of cattle was sighted, looking very much like the placid animals seen in so many pastures. But these beasts were alert and wary, and a long and careful stalk was necessary before they were within range. Two young bulls were selected, the rifles were fired, and the animals fell, while the rest of the herd galloped off.

With wild, triumphant yells our guides fell upon the still-twitching bodies and cut their throats with machetes. Then, much of our horror, the guides cupped their hands to catch the gushing blood and drank it with great relish. The carcasses were skinned and cut into haunches that were slung under poles and carried back, some for the ship's freezer and some for the local people. When we returned to the settlement in Tai-o-hae Bay there was plenty of beef for the entire population there.

The Marquesas are as dramatically beautiful as any group of islands in the Pacific. Their lush valleys are choked with mango, coconut, and breadfruit trees; their many rivers cascade down from mountains that are eternally green from the clouds that cap them every afternoon. Some of them are crowned with great rock pinnacles, like the turrets of some fairytale giants' castles. Once these islands were populated by a proud, virile people, the Vikings of the Pacific. But with the arrival of the white man, their fate was sealed. Who was to blame for this great tragedy? Was it the whalers, who brought smallpox, syphilis, and other diseases? Was it the traders, who brought liquor? Was it the missionaries, who forced the people to cover their nakedness with clothes, which became soaked with the daily rains? Was it the government, which suppressed the people's warlike rites and their wild dances? Most likely, it was a combination of all these factors. We were saddened to see the population of these fertile islands so decimated, their rich valleys almost empty of people, a pathetic contrast to the descriptions of Herman Melville and other early writers.

After visiting several islands in the Marquesas, we headed on toward Tahiti and passed through the Tuamotus. These are a chain of atolls running in a southeast-northwest direction for many hundreds of miles. Being atolls, they were very low-lying, and the first sight of them is the tops of the palms over the horizon. Thus one must be extremely careful navigating among them. We passed by Takaroa at night, and on this occasion I was able to perpetrate one of the worst puns in my career. As we sailed close to the island, which was clearly visible, we caught a whiff of baking bread. I turned to Sheridan and said in solemn tones, "Bakers ahead, sir."

From then on it was a clear run to Tahiti, and one morning we entered the harbor of Papeete on this fabulous island. At that time Tahiti was indeed an unspoiled paradise. The only visits it had from the outside world beside a few itinerant yachts was the Messageries Maritimes ship on its way to New Zealand and Indochina, when the mail was dropped off. This occurred about every three or four weeks and caused great activity in Papeete. Everybody came to town to collect their mail, exchange gossip, and celebrate accordingly.

Sadly, the island has changed greatly and irrevocably since the end of World War II. With the completion of a large international airport, hotels and condominiums began springing up like mushrooms, seemingly overnight. A constant stream of tourist ships followed, so boutiques and souvenir shops were also inevitable. But the greatest changes have come from the French nuclear weapons testing program in the Tuamotu Archipelago. Tahiti became the main base for the program, and hundreds of scientists and technicians arrived, with all their requirements for housing, administration, and research facilities. To accommodate the naval vessels involved in the program, much of the once-beautiful lagoon in front of Papeete was filled in to provide dock facilities. Motu Iti, the lovely little palm-covered islet in the middle of the lagoon, is gone. The relaxed, sleepy atmosphere of the old port of Papeete is no more. There are traffic jams in the busy streets during business hours, and the picturesque weathered buildings along the waterfront have been replaced by glittery modern stores, restaurants, and overnight accommodations. A recent stop I made there convinced me to do all I could to forget the new Tahiti and revel in those sweet memories of a romantic island that will never be again.

Naturally, we were giving no such dismal thoughts to the future of the island as we entered the pass between the reefs into the lagoon. We were relishing the beauty of the white buildings with their mellowed red roofs along the waterfront, against a backdrop of tall green mountains. We picked up a pilot, and with an engine that was still behaving we headed toward the tree-lined waterfront. The pilot told us when to drop the anchor; we then swung the ship around and backed the stern in toward the waterfront. When about ten feet away from the embankment, we ran lines ashore to ancient cannons buried in the greensward. Thus we were moored, and by running a plank across to the shore we had a perfect anchorage. The waterfront was lined with interisland vessels coming from the Tuamotus and other island groups nearby, bringing in their freights of pineapples, pigs, coconuts, vanilla, fish, and other products, as well as passengers.

Along the waterfront street decrepit-looking buses were passing back and forth, with crowded piles of baggage on top. Very often people were hanging outside the bus and even seated on the front. Many were girls with leis of flowers around their necks, and usually there was a good deal of singing and guitar playing in progress.

After we had snugged down the ship, the American consul came on board, and we asked him what the celebrations were for. He looked at us in a puzzled way and informed us that this was a regular working day. We had never seen such gaiety in any other part of the world, but we soon entered into the spirit of it.

For three unattached males we soon discovered the normal practice in Tahiti, which involved attaching oneself to any one of numerous available young ladies, and as long as one remained reasonably faithful to them there was no problem. But as soon as the male visitor departed, the young woman lost no time, having wiped a few tears from her eyes, in attaching herself to the next available male. There was no prostitution, it was all done in the name of love, and it worked out very conveniently for everyone involved. When a ship did come in, all the available young women were lined up along the waterfront waiting to get attached to a newcomer. They were quickly picked up and taken care of until the visitors left. It would be a sad scene as the ship sailed, but broken hearts were very quickly mended and so nobody suffered for long. Aimee happened to be my companion for quite a while; she was a typical young Tahitian girl, quite uninhibited and free. She asked nothing much from me, except my full attendance. It was a shock to me, once, as we were walking hand in hand, when she stopped and, still holding my hand, proceeded to relieve herself, and then we walked on. This was perfectly natural behavior.

I heard a story in Quinn's bar in Papeete told by a half-caste American named Mike, who had lived in the islands almost all his life. His little tale, told in his own words as well as I can remember them, is typical of love in Polynesia and provides as good a picture as any lengthy novel.

"I remember when I was a lad of sixteen," began Mike, "I never did give a damn about the girls. All I liked was sailing, and I spent all my time on the big copra schooners. My one ambition was to have a ship of my own someday.

"Then one day when we were in Mangareva in the Gambiers, I met Mirii on the beach. She'd just come in from fishing on the reef, and her hair was all wet. I guess she was around fifteen, and pretty shy. We just stood looking at each other for a spell, and I forgot all about the schooner I wanted to have someday. Then I went up and took her by the hand, and she didn't seem a bit surprised.

"The upshot of it was, I decided to take her to Tahiti and marry her. So I hid her in among the sacks of copra down in the hold, and when we were two days out I told the skipper. He was pretty mad for a while, but I knew he wouldn't put back, as we were several hundred miles downwind by then. He wasn't a bad guy, and I guess he liked me, even if he did think I was crazy.

"Anyhow, he said he'd take the girl's passage out of my wages and let it go at that. So then he goes below and tells her to come out on deck. I remember I was at the wheel at the time, and I saw her climb out of the hatch. She looked around in a timid kind of way, then she sees me and smiled, and I know she isn't scared anymore.

"And I guess I felt about as good then as I've ever done, as I saw her there with her long hair blowing in the wind, and I knew she belonged to me.

"And you should have seen her eyes pop when we came through the pass here, and she saw all the houses and the ships and the dock. She thought it was the grandest sight in all the world."

Mike gave a short laugh.

"But we never did get around to being married. Three days after we got in some Frenchman picked her up, and she went off with him. I often used to see her afterward, when we came to town. She was always along the waterfront with the other girls, just looking for anybody she could find. That's the way they all are down here."

A yacht came in soon after we arrived and one of the men on board was from Omaha. Little did he know that *Omaha* was the Tahitian word for urinating, and so he became the butt of everyone in Tahiti once he announced his origin. He never lived it down.

We had a good alibi for staying in Tahiti for several months, if that were necessary. It was the season for hurricanes farther west in the Pacific. Therefore, it made good sense to remain in Tahiti and the neighboring islands. We needed to scrub the bottom of the ship and so we had her hauled out for a while in the little shipyard at Fareute Point, and in the meantime we rented a small shack outside of town for five dollars a month. The five dollars included the services of a girl who did our marketing for us. We spent a month in this little shack before the ship was launched again and we could move back on board. I doubt if five dollars would last a visitor more than two minutes in these days.

In the meantime, we sailed to some of the neighboring islands, making friends in Mooréa, Raiatea, Tahaa, and Bora Bora. While we were in Papeete, a forty-five-foot yacht named *Hurricane* came in, manned by two Iowans, Ray Kauffman and Gerry Mefferd. With them was a Mexican named Hector as crewman. We very quickly made friends with them and were amazed to find that neither of the Iowans had seen the sea before they sailed out of the Mississippi. But they were good seamen and had a very fine vessel that they had built in Pascagoula. So we were able to cruise with them through many of the island groups of the Pacific, arranging to meet up in port after a passage from the last group of islands.

We were coming close to the time of our departure, the hurricane season being over by the beginning of 1936, when a tragedy of sorts struck. It happened this way: as I mentioned before, while in Gatun Lake in Panama I had caught a medium-sized boa constrictor that quickly became quite easy to handle and in fact appeared to enjoy our company. Sometimes I would be sitting at the wheel and he would coil around my body, apparently appreciating the warmth of my skin. I kept him in a wooden box with a wire top on the foredeck. By feeding him a dead bird or mouse about once a month, he did very well. I became very fond of Egbert; he was an amiable snake.

We had made arrangements with the local Chinese baker to deliver bread early every morning. This was brought aboard by the baker's small boy, and the bread was placed at the head of the companionway. One morning when I arose to pick up the bread, I happened to glance forward and much to my horror found the lid was off Egbert's box. I realized then that the little boy, being curious, had tiptoed forward to look into the box, seen the snake, and run away in terror. I looked around for Egbert but could not find him. I searched as thoroughly as I could and finally concluded that he must have crawled up into the folded sails. I hoped that I would find him later. That evening I was sitting in Quinn's bar enjoying a quiet beer when a crowd of people came in with much excited babble in a mixture of Tahitian and bad French. I was not particularly listening to what they were talking about until I heard the one word, "serpent," and realized that they were discussing Egbert.

I soon found out what had happened. When the interisland vessels came into port the crews and passengers found it more convenient to move ashore rather than stay on a overcrowded ship. They merely rolled themselves in a sheet and went to sleep on the sidewalk. It appears that one old woman, who must have been having a bad dream, opened her eyes and rolled over, and there was Egbert in front of her. She gave a cry of horror, for the only snake the Tahitians knew of was the one the priests had told them about, which was the Devil, who had tempted Eve to partake of the apple. She began to wail that the Devil had come to Tahiti. Everybody else woke up, and they regarded the poor innocent Egbert in terror. The lamentations must have been quite noisy, for eventually one of the local gendarmes arrived to find out what the hullaballoo was all about, and there was Egbert surrounded by a circle of wailing islanders. With great courage the gendarme grabbed a machete, and poor Egbert was chopped into many pieces. The following day his remains were exhibited in the window of the local drugstore, and for a while it was not clear how the Devil had come to Tahiti. Eventually it became known that it was the Americans on the yacht that had committed this foul deed. From then on we were regarded with great suspicion, and we realized that it was time to leave.

Before we did head westward, however, we decided to take advantage of a piece of advice given to us by an old sailor who had spent many years in the islands. He suggested that we should take along rum as a gift to people we would be visiting in the lonelier islands farther westward. He pointed out that we would be wandering through island groups such as the Solomons and New Hebrides, where the local planters and government administrators led very lonely lives, and that a bottle of rum was a great way to establish friendships in return for local hospitality. Moreover, he told us that since we were a ship, we could buy rum in bond, as ship's stores, and that if we did so it would be extremely cheap. This indeed turned out to be true. The local Tahitian rum was of very fine quality and when purchased in bond it only cost about fifteen U.S. cents a liter. This was an opportunity too good to be missed. So we ordered a supply of rum but then, to our amazement, found that the smallest quantity we could obtain in bond was a 220-liter barrel.

The barrel arrived, and it was monstrous; it took up most of the deck space and was in the way of the sails. There was no way in the world that we could cross the Pacific with this enormous bulk on deck, and it was of course impossible to get it down the companionway. So the obvious thing to do was to bottle it as soon as we left Papeete. This required making a deal with the local Chinese trader for 220 one-liter bottles and the necessary corks. We then had a great inspiration. We would sail over to the nearby island of Mooréa, anchor in quiet waters at the head of the bay, and decant the rum from the barrel into the bottles.

We anchored in Opunohu Bay and brought the bottles on deck, looked at the barrel, and then began to puzzle how to get the rum out of the barrel into the bottles. There was no point in trying to pour it out of the barrel; it would have spilled all over the deck, and certainly more of it would have gone overboard than into the bottles.

Some friends of ours ashore were consulted. They thought for a while, and then one of them had an inspiration: "We have an old enema tube; how would that do as a siphon?"

"Splendid!" we said.

So the enema tube was brought aboard, the bung was removed, the tube was inserted into the barrel, and to get the rum to flow a suck at the other end of the tube was necessary. Thus the bottling operation began. But every time we filled a bottle we had to take a suck at the tube. After three days of bottling, the condition of the bottlers perhaps can be imagined. But somehow we did finally get all the rum into the bottles and then we could rid ourselves of that enormous barrel, return the enema tube to our kindly friends, and stow the bottles as best we could. Most of them went into the bilge; others were stowed into every conceivable cranny on board. But as we sailed westward across the Pacific and the ship rolled we would hear the musical clanking of the bottles as they rolled together. We had made it a very firm principle that there was to be no drinking at sea, but when we came into port, it was a different matter. We did find the rum an extremely useful gift and a good way to establish friendships. It was excellent rum, and it took almost two years before the last bottle was consumed.

From Mooréa we sailed westward to the islands known as Les Îles Sous le Vent (Islands under the Wind): Raiatea, Tahaa, Huaheine, and Bora Bora, all equally lovely. At Bora Bora we met up with *Hurricane* again and agreed on a friendly race to the next island, which was to be Tongareva, or Penrhyn as it is sometimes called. This was an atoll, and one of the inducements was the possibility of diving for pearls. We sailed at the same time but soon lost sight of each other.

By this time we had another shipmate on board. In Tahiti we had been joined by Lewis Hirshon, a wealthy young American who had decided to settle down in Tahiti when he had fallen in love with a beautiful half-Polynesian, half-Maori girl of royal blood. He realized that if he were to marry her, he would have committed himself to making Tahiti his permanent home. When we came along, this might have been a good opportunity to find out the depths of his love for Eugenie, and it was obvious as he sailed with us that he was yearning to get back to her. In the meantime, he had given her a first-class ticket to Paris, and he was terrified of her being picked up by some wealthy boulevardier, with him losing her forever. Torn as he was between sailing with us and a life with Eugenie, he was eventually to leave us. Since, when we reached Fiji, *Hurricane* was heading down for Australia, he decided to sail with her and catch up with Eugenie as quickly as possible. In the meantime, he was a splendid companion and shipmate, and I developed a great affection for him.

It was Easter Sunday when we arrived off the atoll of Tongareva, although we were unaware of that fact at the time. The islanders were all crowded into the church for morning service when a small boy, who was not concentrating on the sermon, sighted our sails outside the passage into the lagoon and gave a loud cry of "Ehippy!" As one, the congregation rose to their feet and dashed out of the church and headed for the waterfront. The men, still in their Sunday finery, piled into every available craft, mostly dugout canoes, and hurried out to meet us and pilot us in. They crowded onto our decks and swarmed all over the ship, excited as children at this unexpected visit.

As we entered the pass, we realized how essential an engine was in such a situation. As with all atolls, the ocean swells breaking over the reefs pour into the lagoon, continuously building up the water level there. This causes a current to be flowing constantly out of any breaks in the line of reefs, and therefore an engine is vital to enter such a place. To attempt it under sail alone, unless the wind was very strong and from a favorable direction, would be the poorest kind of seamanship. On this occasion, the engine behaved, and with several dozen pilots to con us in, we entered the lagoon in great style and anchored off the little settlement of Omoka.

Next morning we were invited to accompany one of the pearling vessels and had an enjoyable day diving for *pipi* pearls. These pearls are tiny but very beautiful, coming from a small oyster occurring in fairly shallow water. They are not of any great value but are mainly prized by Indian maharajas and other Oriental potentates for decorating drapes on their processional elephants and horses. So we dove happily, bringing up piles of *pipi* shells and occasionally finding a pearl, to our great excitement. These little pearls come in a variety of colors, ranging all the way from black through white, though most of them are copper-colored, orange, or pale yellow, and to my mind they are much more attractive than the more valuable white pearls, which are found in a different, much larger species of oyster.

A few days later *Hurricane* came in, and we had a joyous reunion with them and then decided on our next stop, which would be the Samoan group of islands. By this time the two Fahnestock brothers were having problems with their eyesight, due to the glare of the tropical sun. So when we reached Pango Pango on Tutuila, which is an American island, they consulted the local U.S. Navy surgeon. He recommended a week's rest for them in darkened rooms while he treated them. This left Lewis and me to remain on the ship. We were not too delighted at that prospect, as there was little to be seen around the harbor of Pango Pango. We wanted to see more of the island, so we decided to start strolling around it, following the coastal road. We had heard a great deal about the hospitality of the Samoan islanders, how each village had a special hut and they were always ready to receive visitors. So we began our leisurely stroll, stopping off at small villages, much to our enjoyment.

We reached one village at the eastern end of the island, and the chief had apparently learned of the war between Italy and Ethiopia which was then, in early 1936, in progress. As we sat around the circular *fale* in the evening with our backs propped against the roof supports, he began to question us about the war. Now, we hadn't read a newspaper for many months and had only heard vaguely of the war, but we were able to describe the modern machinery of combat, such as tanks, planes, shells, and bullets. The chief and his family were fascinated.

Next morning we were planning to proceed on our way when the chief approached us to ask if we would be willing to stay one more night and said if we were, he would call in the elders from the neighboring villages. They would organize a feast for us with dances and, moreover, would initiate us into the local clan. Since we had no particular plans this sounded like a fine way to spend another day in the village, so we readily agreed. During the course of the day Lewis and I had plenty of opportunity to rehearse and dig into the depths of our imaginations, to make our stories of the war sound as fascinating as possible for these war-minded people.

When the evening began, we sat around the main *fale* in the village, and they began to serve us kava.

Kava is a drink prepared from the root of a shrub of the pepper family; it is very often chewed by the local virgins and spit into a bowl and mixed with water. In this instance we were not sure whether the virgins did indeed do the job or whether it was simply macerated, but nevertheless, this strange drink, which reminds one of licorice-flavored dishwater and has about that color, was not unpleasant. It has an odd effect on one, perhaps partly due to the position one has to take all evening, sitting on the ground with legs crossed and tucked in under the body. The effect is remarkable: it does not affect the mind at all and in that sense is nonintoxicating. It does, however, have a very strange effect on the lower regions. The legs become boneless and as if made of rubber, and so when we rose to our feet, we staggered around in a most awkward fashion. In fact, the entire nether regions are more or less paralyzed. Whenever the kava was offered in a wooden bowl we had to knock it back, so in the course of the evening we consumed quite a good deal of it.

The audience was fascinated; they asked many questions in their broken English, and we were able to satisfy them as best we could, going into very lurid descriptions of that particular war. At the end of the session the feast began, with the pig roasted in the hot coals and the breadfruit and the other vegetables served on banana leaves by the village maidens. Following the feast there was a dance performance by these beautiful young women. This was the so-called sitting siva, where they squat on the ground and undulate their arms in a way that is remindful of a wind rippling down a pennant. It is a most graceful dance, and the singing is also very attractive.

Watching the swaying bodies, the long, glossy black Polynesian hair, and the lithe bodies of these girls, it was a little hard for us to remain seated, but we managed to restrain ourselves.

Following this, the chief indicated that we would be initiated into the local clan, and then we saw a man approaching us with a coconut shell bowl with two sticks in it and some evil-looking black liquid. Then it dawned upon us what was to happen. "Good God," Lew whispered to me, "they are going to tattoo us." At that time Samoan males were tattooed from navel to knees. It was a long and painful process, taking months, and was done on a piecemeal basis. This time, fortunately, they only intended to tattoo us on the arm. They signed to us to lie down on our bellies, removing our shirts, and the man with the bowl of black liquid approached us. At the end of one stick and at right angles to it was a shark's tooth. This was dipped in the black liquid and then held over the skin, and the other stick was used to rap the stick with the shark's tooth into the skin. By just maintaining the correct pressure, the tooth did not penetrate all the layers of skin, just the top few. It did not take very long, and although during the next several weeks our arms swelled up and turned various colors of the rainbow, it eventually cleared up, scabs fell off, and we were then tattooed for life. Perhaps I will someday end up as a lampshade.

The final act came when we were given fine woven mats to sleep on, and as an ultimate gesture of Samoan hospitality, village virgins were assigned to sleep beside each of us. It was, however, an empty gesture, as the kava had done its work, and by next morning the two virgins were still intact.

6

Cannibals and Cockatoos

We continued on our leisurely walk around the island, and now that we had learned how best to entertain our Samoan hosts, we gave repeat performances of the epic story of "Italy versus Ethiopia." By the time we returned to the ship in Pango Pango Harbor, we felt like experts on the history of that particular war. Fortunately for our egos, we did not run into anyone who might have disputed our extravagantly imagined tales.

By the end of two weeks, the two brothers were much recovered, though Bruce, who had the worst case of painful eyes, had to wear dark glasses for many months when exposed to the tropical sun.

When we left the Samoan Islands we also left Polynesia and began entering Melanesian waters. The first group was the Fijis. The islands of the so-called Lau archipelago were very lovely and enjoyable; but when we reached Suva, trouble developed. Suva was a fairly large port, and at that time it had many bars. The two brothers found this much to their enjoyment, and so there was a fair amount of drunkenness and unpleasant altercations when they returned on board. So when *Hurricane* came into port, Lewis made up his mind to join her, as he no longer wished to sail on *Director*. This was a great loss to me; he had been the best of shipmates.

Now we were in Melanesia, with islands that had a reputation for wild people and dense jungle. We would need to be very careful in dealing with the local people. While planters and government administrators certainly would be glad to see us, in other areas we might very easily run into trouble, since there were many hostile people ahead of us. We were advised to take along a very important item of trade goods, namely, stick tobacco. This is a pencillike stick of very tightly packed leaf tobacco, an excellent means of making friends with the natives. We did have plenty of warning about the possibility of meeting hostile peoples. Recruiters had very often taken these natives to work in the Queensland sugar plantations, where they had been badly treated and very often cheated, and therefore they maintained a hostile attitude toward whites. So with these warnings we sailed out of Suva Harbor, headed for the New Hebrides Islands.

When we entered at Efate Harbor, where the main administrative offices were located, we found a very confusing situation. These islands were administered by what was known as a Condominium Government, whimsically referred to as the Pandemonium Government. There were representatives of two of the colonial empires, France and Britain, and instead of having one immigration official to deal with, we had two. This kind of duplication occurred in all offices in the New Hebrides at that time. Now, the New Hebrides Islands have been granted their independence and are officially the nation of Vanuatu.

When we reached the island of Espíritu Santo, Bruce and I decided to hunt for some fruit pigeons, as we were short of food and this would be a welcome change from weevil-infested spaghetti and ketchup. Landing on a sandy beach, we entered the dense forest and soon had shot several birds with our ancient twelve-gauge shot-gun. It was eerie in the darkness of the dense vegetation, and we had an odd sense of danger, though we knew we should not venture very far from the beach. Emerging into a more semiopen scrubland area, we were surprised to find a narrow trail that appeared to have been made by humans. By this time, we were sufficiently nervous to decide to head back for our landing beach and the security of our vessel.

But suddenly out stepped a figure in front of us. It was a native, naked except for a G-string around his middle. In his mop of bushy hair was a rooster tail feather, and under one arm was tucked a Snyder smooth-bore rifle. These weapons were much prized in the New Hebrides and Solomon Islands and were a symbol of manhood. The natives would work for a year on an Australian sugar plantation to earn one. Polished to paper thinness, a gun would probably burst apart, with the loss of a few fingers, if it was fired.

The man glowered at us in what we felt was a somewhat unfriendly attitude, and while we stood nonplussed half a dozen more appeared out of the bush, so we were surrounded. They signed for us to follow them up the trail, and after some hesitation we felt this was our only recourse. We had been escorted uphill for about an hour when we came to a clearing where the settlement was located. It consisted of a collection of low lean-tos of palm thatch, into which one would need to enter on all fours. A crowd collected around us, and we did our best to smile in a friendly manner when the chief approached us. We could tell he was the chief by his gray hair and beard and the band of colored pants buttons around his neck. From one of his pierced, drooping earlobes he produced the stub of a blackened clay pipe, pointing to it. At once we realized, with some relief, that he was desperate for tobacco and this was why we had been more or less kidnapped. Fortunately, we had always made sure that we carried some tobacco with us in our backpack, and when we produced a few sticks and presented them his face brightened into a broad grin, with much display of teeth stained black by betelnut juice.

Friendship was then quickly established, and to show his gratitude the chief shouted an order, and about eight naked females lined up in the background. This was an obvious invitation for us to take our pick, but once we had looked them over we politely declined; they were not the most attractive creatures, as most of them had skin scaly with yaws. So we settled for a small, squealing pig, tethered by one hind leg. We were escorted back to the beach, and as soon as our escort was out of sight, we released the pig and wished him luck. We did not have the heart to butcher him.

The currency in these primitive islands was "tooth belong pig." This was a circle of the lower front teeth of the pig. By knocking out the upper teeth, the lower ones were allowed to grow and form a circle, and the more perfect the circle, the more perfect the teeth. We were told that three of these would purchase a virgin, but again we decided we would prefer to keep the teeth as a souvenir of our visit to these primitive islands. Little did I know that years later I would be back in these same areas during World War II, but that they would then be unrecognizable. Where formerly had been heavy jungle and savage people there would now be acres of ammunition dumps, airstrips, and barracks buildings as staging areas for the U.S. offensive westward.

We did not stay much longer in the New Hebrides but proceeded on to the Solomons, first stopping at the southeastern end of the archipelago at a lovely little island named Santa Anna in the Owa Raha group. Here a German trader named Kuper had married a native woman and they had produced children, and it was my good fortune to meet one of these children during World War II, who had become a very important coast watcher.

Cruising through the Solomons, we stopped at the Santa Cruz Islands. The island Ndeni had an excellent harbor, and we found the natives quite friendly, although living under extremely primitive conditions. I came to know the chief, named Mepula, very well, and since we remained there for a couple of weeks, he invited me ashore to a *kaikai*, a feast. By this time I had learned some pidgin English. Although it was a very primitive language, consisting of two hundred–odd English words, they were used for naming any item that attracted their interest. When I attended this *kaikai*, it involved squatting around a large fire, with big hunks of bloody meat that were tossed into the fire until they turned black and were then fished out with a pointed stick. I was invited to help myself, which I did. I selected the least repulsive-looking piece of meat, waited awhile for it to cook, and finally drew it out. I found it particularly chewy and quite unattractive, but I managed to gulp it down somehow, since I did not want to offend my host. I was curious to know what kind of meat it was and assumed it was the meat of one of the feral cattle from the previous plantation. So I turned to Mepula and in my best pidgin English asked, "What name this fella bullamacow?" The response was, "This no fella bullamacow, this fella long pig." Meaning, of course, that I had eaten human flesh. I did not feel very comfortable about this, but since I had not been introduced to the gentleman in question, I managed to keep the flesh down.

Pidgin is a fascinating language, and in those days it required a great deal of ingenuity to describe something new. For example, the words for glove were "trousers belong finger" and for brassiere "hammock belong titty." The airplane, which was seen very rarely, was, "auto belong Jesus Christ." I remember hearing a planter order his boy to bring in some honey, saying, "Boy, you catch 'em shit belong bee." But perhaps, the prize must go to the word for piano: "box, you fight 'em teeth belong him, belly belong him cry out." Since those early days the pidgin vocabulary has expanded and the language has been formalized, so it is now the official tongue in the Solomons and Papua New Guinea. Even the Bible has been translated into pidgin, and there is a pidgin dictionary.

As we wandered farther westward through the rest of the Solomon group it became obvious that the two Fahnestock brothers were not well. They had contracted what we diagnosed as malaria, and although Atabrine had already been developed, it didn't seem to be doing them much good. We slowly came to the realization that we must eventually get out of the tropics.

We reached the little island of Samarai at the eastern tip of Papua and were able to tie up at the dock. The Fahnestocks went on an evening's carouse at the local bars. At that time Samarai was a center for gold prospecting in the islands of the Louisiade Archipelago, and there were many rough and tough characters in the area. I never found out the full details of what occurred in the bar that the brothers visited, but they ran into trouble in the usual way when they had too much to drink. It was usually Bruce who initiated these incidents, as he became particularly aggressive.

Somehow he entered into an argument with one of these characters and ended up by throwing his drink in the man's face. It must have been a pretty potent drink, because it temporarily blinded the man. The two brothers ran out of the bar and quickly headed for the ship, with some of the diggers in pursuit. I was asleep at the time; they roused me up and in desperate voices told me, "Denny, cast off at once; we've got to go!" Still half-asleep I took in the dock lines, while Bruce started the engine, which, fortunately, was in operating condition at the time. As we moved away from the dock, some angry men came down to the waterside yelling threats and obscenities as we steamed out just in time to avoid what might have been a very difficult situation. I learned some of the details later and was certainly grateful for not being directly involved in this kind of unnecessary confrontation. I cannot think of any tougher group of men than Australian diggers, and these ones were out for blood.

We continued on toward Australia and New Guinea, stopping along the south coast of New Guinea and making a formal entry at Port Moresby. It was then quite a small settlement, but nevertheless the seat of government for this great island. While there, I was befriended by the local His Majesty's Justice of the Peace, who asked me if I knew the whereabouts of the well-known movie actor Errol Flynn. Denying any knowledge of the man, I inquired why the interest? I then learned a rather shocking tale. It seems that long before Flynn became a film star, he and another man were short-term partners in a plantation in New Guinea. They hired a team of the local natives to work the plantation for them and at the end of a year paid the workers off with pennies they had covered with silver paint and had then skipped out of the country. My friend the judge, therefore, had a warrant out for their arrest, but it as very unlikely that the two scoundrels would ever show their faces here again.

We sailed on through the Arafura Sea. Here we were becalmed for quite a long period. There were seven days when we could barely move, and dust from the Australian desert settled on the water, so the ship looked as if she was sitting in an ocean of sand. The decks became so hot the pitch boiled in the deck seams, and even at night it was hard to sleep because of the heat. So it was a great relief when finally the breeze came, the sand disappeared, and we moved on our way.

There was at this period another unpleasant situation on board. Somehow we had been invaded by cockroaches, but not the small brown creature one finds in a city like New York. These were huge dark brown creatures locally known as "mahogany birds." They managed to hide during the day, but at night they emerged from crevices in the woodwork and were extremely active. If one was to turn on a flashlight at night there would be dozens of them scuttling away. We also found that while we were asleep they liked to eat the dead skin off our feet, which, naturally, were covered with callouses now. We found that one way to kill them was to set out a glass of rum. In the morning we would find as many as half a dozen of them in the glass, quite dead, but apparently happy to die in this way. However many of these "rum traps" we set out, there were always plenty more cockroaches. We did not seem to be able to make any dent in their numbers. They got into the food if any was left out and this gave it a very unpleasant taste and odor, so they were not the most welcome of shipmates.

We stopped at the Tanimbar Islands, and here we encountered some natives who had made pets of a local member of the parrot family named Goffin's cockatoo. It only occurs in this particular group of islands. I was infatuated with these birds. We already had small lories and other delightful birds on board, but these cockatoos had a special appeal. They were very tame and affectionate, and for a few sticks of tobacco we took on three of these small white cockatoos. Little did I know the important part that they would play in my future.

Our next destination was the Timor Laut group of islands in the Arafura Sea. In consulting the pilot book we found that Selaru was the port of entry. We anchored off a little native settlement one evening, but although we waited quite a long time, no official came to us, so we finally rowed ashore and tried to show someone our papers, but everybody shunned us in a rather hostile way. The largest building in the settlement must surely be the residence of the port official. So we went there and finally this elderly man in a ragged shirt came out and pointed to himself and said the one word: "Rajah." So this was the rajah, not the type of rajah we had expected at all. We tried to offer him our papers, but he backed off and signed to us to go back to the ship. His gestures were unmistakable, so this we did, somewhat puzzled by the inhospitable reception we had been given. We went back on board and turned in.

Early next morning there was a bump alongside, and upon awakening we found a dozen barefoot military men climbing aboard with their rifles pointed at us in a very threatening way. We had no recourse but to follow their directions. They signed us to pull up the anchor and head to one of the larger islands across the passage. There was no way of convincing these people that we were harmless, and it soon dawned upon us why we had been treated so inhospitably. They pointed to our diving helmet and muttered the one word "Yapan," and we then realized that they had taken us for Japanese shell poachers, who were then exploiting many of the reefs in Indonesian waters for *trocas* shell, from which shirt buttons were made. When the anchor was up, they signed to us to start the engine and proceed over to the port of Saumlakki. This we did. And although we tried to establish a friendly basis with these people, they were still quite hostile. They insisted we were Japanese, and even when we showed them the stars and stripes they shook their heads and did not even recognize it.

Upon our anchoring off Saumlakki, a high official came aboard, but he, too, was puzzled as to what we were doing in these waters. We again proffered our papers, and he took them ashore, since he was unable to read them himself. When he returned he had with him an old Dutch priest who could speak a little English, and my high school French was much more understandable to him. When we had convinced him that we were entirely harmless and had the officials search the ship and they saw no sign of any shell on our vessel, they realized that they were mistaken in thinking us Japanese poachers. We showed him the pilot book, which indicated that Selaru was the port of entry, and it was explained to us that for the past twenty years Saumlakki on Timor Laut Island had been the port of entry. Once this matter was cleared up we were regarded as harmless but possibly eccentric visitors and the attitude changed. We were soon loaded with fruit and fish, although they were still puzzled by our mission. But we were finally able to clear up the whole matter by identifying ourselves under the one term "Students"; this they accepted and all was well.

We were now very low on funds, and there was no possibility of any more arriving until we reached Manila. Due as much as anything to bad management and an overindulgence in liquid refreshment, we were reduced to feeding on weevily spaghetti, doused with ketchup. We tried to make pancakes out of maggoty flour and condensed milk, and we were short of so many other things, too, that could have made life easier on board. But there was just no hope of renewing our supplies for a while. We did manage to trade some tobacco for fruit when we came to inhabited islands, and this I'm sure helped protect us from any of the symptoms of scurvy. But otherwise the food was unspeakably unappetizing and often bad.

It was now the beginning of December, and our good and steadfast old friend the trade wind was definitely dying. Our passage to the big island of Timor was a struggle against calms and westerly squalls, beset very often by thunderstorms and buckets of rain. Sometimes waterspouts were dancing all around us, and sometimes we sat becalmed beneath a sun that burned down on us with relentless fury. One wind-forsaken evening we drifted into the little harbor of Dili, which is at the Portuguese end of the island, the other half being a part of what was the Netherlands East Indies. The waterfront was lined with old pastel-tinted buildings half-hidden by an avenue of great spreading banyan trees and a frequent scarlet blaze of flamboyants. As we dropped anchor the light offshore breeze died and the air grew dense and still.

Suddenly a horrendous squeal came from the gloom of one of the banyan trees. It was a signal that brought forth an immediate Devil's chorus of answering squeals, until the whole night was filled with the unearthly noise. Over the trees we could see a cloud of dim shapes wheeling and flitting like a host of evil witches. They were flying foxes, the big East Indian fruit bats that during the daytime hang with folded wings in the branches like strangely shaped fruits. At dusk at a given signal from the leader they awaken to make the nights of Dili hideous with their dismal cries. After circling around a while they head off for the interior to do their night's feeding on jungle fruit.

Our water tanks were nearly empty, but when we asked the port authorities for water they were embarrassed to tell us that they had been unable to pay the man who laid down the pipes to the end of the dock and he had been churlish enough to dig them all up and take them away. We then protested that the pilot book indicated that water was supplied to shipping at Dili, and if this was no longer so, we would have to report it to the U.S. Hydrographic Office. This threat turned the fussy little port captain's face pale. "Very well then," he said at last with a visible effort, "we'll have the waterpipes put down again." A bag of money was dispatched to the pipe man with a request for him to hurry up with the work. A gang of native prisoners was soon at work digging a deep trench across the road, while others staggered beneath the burden of sections of huge iron pipe.

Two days later the work was completed and the port captain proudly intimated that *Director* could move alongside the dock to water the ship. We did so, taking on our modest few hundred gallons, for which we were with much ceremony handed the official-looking document that was our water bill. The whole affair was settled when we solemnly paid the sum of eighty cents Mex., twenty-four cents in U.S. currency.

Besides the few Portuguese officials residing in Dili and some American mining engineers, who were making a geological survey of the interior, there was another class of workingman in Portuguese Timor. They were the "Deportados," sorry-looking figures exiled from their homeland for crimes ranging from murder to the making of a injudicious speech in favor of Communism. Never again would they see the noisy streets of Lisbon or smell the pungent reek of the sardine villages. Sad-eyed, they lived on in faraway Timor. Many of them, for want of something to occupy their thoughts, took for wives the dirty, scrawny native women. Each week these men had to report to the police, and every month they all received from the government the princely sum of $27.00 Mex. ($8.00 U.S.). This of course was not enough to support them, so they had to seek whatever jobs they could find. Some of them were seen working beside the naked Timorese on the roads. A few more fortunate found themselves better posts as bakers, engineers, and carpenters. But at best they were a fever-stricken, brokenhearted, pathetic band.

After leaving Timor, we began heading up north through the Indonesian archipelago stopping at many islands. But the winds were fitful and currents were unpredictable, so we had difficulty navigating through these waters, particularly since the charts were not very reliable. Sometimes at night it would be alarming to hear the roar of breakers at a distance where, according to our navigation, we should have been well offshore. And then we would hear these tumbling waters coming closer and closer and finally we would be surrounded by tossing waves and we realized that this was some kind of riptide where two strong currents were meeting. After a while the turbulence would pass and the ship would settle down again on an even keel. But for the first few experiences of these strange riptides we were filled with anxiety.

We also passed through avenues of waterspouts at times, and these, too, were alarming, but fortunately, we never were particularly close to one of them. We stopped at several spice islands and were sorely tempted to take on more birds, but we felt that this would hurt the feelings of our Tanimbar Island cockatoos, so we refrained. Perhaps it was just as well we did, for the cockatoos themselves were quite enough to give us trouble with their constant chewing of the woodwork. At length we reached Zamboanga at the southern tip of the large island of Mindanao in the southern Philippines.

By this time we were a somewhat disreputable-looking vessel. The sides of our hull were stained with rust from the chain plates, our paint was sadly lacking, and our sails were somewhat bedraggled. So we were rather ashamed of ourselves when a large motor yacht, over one hundred feet long, anchored near us. She was very smart and impeccably maintained; a crew of white-jacketed sailors was running around the decks, performing whatever duties were involved. From the stern flew the Japanese meatball flag. A launch came over after a while, and a smart-looking officer questioned us as to where we had been and what we were doing. He was obviously interested in our cockatoos, and when we explained where we had obtained them he was even more interested and asked if the ship's owner could come over to see us. We naturally agreed and as soon as he left we began cleaning up the ship as best we could.

It should be mentioned at this point that one of the problems we had with the cockatoos was their insatiable desire to chew the woodwork along our companionway entrance, stripping off slivers of wood with their beaks. Another problem was in my use of colored pencils for my sketches. Whenever I mislaid these pencils, the cockatoos would pounce on them and split them with their beaks, holding the pencils in one foot while they did this. They apparently relished the contents, which would pass right through them and end up on the white cabin top, which was soon decorated with large blotches of purple, blue, pink, green, and other varied colors.

Eventually the aristocratic Japanese gentleman who owned the yacht came over and began asking us, in excellent English, what we had been doing and where we had been, expressing a great interest in our cockatoos. He explained that he was collecting specimens for Emperor Hirohito's private zoo, so now we had a God-given opportunity to get rid of our cockatoos and at the same time find for them the most desirable home in the world. Surely they would receive better treatment in the Imperial Palace grounds than anywhere else.

So we very gladly presented these cockatoos to the Japanese gentleman, and he, bowing from the waist and hissing through his teeth in gratitude, took them with him, upon which our poor old ship gave a sigh of relief. Before he left, he informed us that when we reached Manila we would receive appropriate acknowledgment of our gift. This indeed did occur when we reached Manila some weeks later. A large launch came out from the Japanese embassy, which still existed then in early 1937, and we were presented with a formidable-looking document informing us that we had presented the emperor with these birds. There was also a clipping in the local English-language newspaper describing the incident. These papers I kept as souvenirs, little realizing that they would become important to me later.

By this time it was obvious that my two shipmates must get out of the tropics. The attacks of malaria were becoming more frequent, so we accepted the advice of every doctor we knew to head up the China coast. We sailed over to the Chinese mainland, left our vessel in good hands at Kowloon, and from there traveled northward and finally reached Peking. We were able to rent a small house, and from then on my shipmates were receiving the proper treatment for their malaria.

When we left *Director*, we little realized we would never see her again; we never did learn her ultimate fate. We did hear later that she was taken over by the Japanese. What use they could have for her was hard to understand. We tried to trace her, but her fate is still a mystery. And as for Tiger and Jose, the parrot, I had to part with them also. A kindly couple who ran a boardinghouse in Kowloon were delighted to take care of them, and subsequently, when I tried through a friend to recover Tiger, they refused to give her up. I could not blame them. But I often wonder what the ultimate fate was of that beloved little animal, since Hong Kong and Kowloon were captured by the Japanese a couple of years later.

Peking was then a very beautiful city, full of excitement and interest for me. I would wander the streets, which were named after the trades existing there, such as Embroidery Street, Jade Street, Silver Street, Copper Street, Painting Street, and so on, and enjoy the beautiful hand-produced products available there. In the small shops one found craftsmen working diligently in exquisite detail fashioning articles of ivory, jade, and other materials without any pressing production date. I remember watching a man working on a large jade vase encrusted with birds, butterflies, and flowers and hung with chains, all cut out of the living jade. He told me that his father before him had started the vase many years ago and he, now a middle-aged man, was convinced that he would be unable to complete it in his lifetime. But he expected his son to continue the work after he was gone. It was this kind of dedication to the beautification of materials that is an integral part of the Chinese artisan's skills. The silverware and the copperware that I saw were entrancing, and the embroidery, much of it coming from ancient ceremonial robes, was startlingly beautiful and done with great attention to detail. These panels were then fashioned into women's jackets sold for a few dollars. In spite of my shortage of cash, I could not resist buying some of these for the family.

I do believe that going into the art shops and seeing some of the exquisite paintings of birds on show there influenced my own painting in terms of the amount of detail I was able to give them. There were other charming aspects of Peking in those days; one was the great flocks of pigeons constantly circling overhead. The Chinese had developed tiny bamboo pipe organs, strapped to the pigeons' backs, and as they soared overhead the air rushing through the pipes would produce beautiful music. Another delight was to see people with their caged birds walking them through the streets, and if ever a procession came by, the birds would be held up so that they could see the procession, in the belief that the more experiences they had, the richer would be the song, as the birds recounted their experiences at a later time.

Now there are no more flocks of pigeons soaring over the cities of China, and there are no more pet birds. Wild birds are scarce. The Mao government decreed that birds were competing with humans for food, so they were hunted down. This has resulted in the proliferation of insect pests, so farmers are committed to the drastic use of chemical pesticides.

The delights of the old city of Peking were soon to come to an end. The Japanese military in north China were already present in great numbers. The Kwantung army was conducting maneuvers there—an odd situation, but nevertheless no one seemed to object; the Japanese were merely waiting for the right incident so that the hostilities could begin. From within the Japanese embassy we frequently heard strange warlike sounds. It was the roaring of the troops being prepared for battles to come, and it all started one morning in early July, at the Marco Polo Bridge, a little way outside Peking. The Japanese claimed that they had been fired upon by Chinese soldiers, and sporadic fighting ensued outside the city walls. I ventured out one day and found several wounded Chinese soldiers and dying horses lying in the road. We were able to help a few of the men and brought them to a hospital, but fortunately the local Chinese warlords sold out, so Peking was not attacked and its beauty thus destroyed. The Japanese marched in with great triumph and quickly took over the city.

In the meantime, American authorities were anxious to evacuate all their citizens, and my two shipmates were eager to go. I could not blame them since they were given the opportunity to, but as I was still a British subject I was left behind. The situation was rather grim. I had very little money, and it seemed as if the war was spreading like a forest fire fanned by high winds across north China at terrifying speed. Shanghai and Tientsin fell, and the war moved farther southward. The Chinese were poorly organized, and local warlords, one after another, sold out, so resistance collapsed. So where could I go? The British were not seemingly concerned about the welfare of their people. Perhaps they had too many business commitments in the country to abandon everything in which they had been so long involved. In the meantime the Japanese troops were becoming more and more arrogant, and the few Westerners that remained in the city were being treated with less and less respect. There were several incidents of beatings and other abuses, and certainly I had little reason for remaining. The whole question, of course, was how to get out.

It was then that the thought occurred to me that the incident of the three cockatoos might possibly be helpful to me. I bore that in mind as I wandered the streets. It was just another case of the good luck that always seemed to follow me when I encountered a young Japanese officer of lowly rank who was anxious to try out his English. He was obviously a well-educated man and was very proud of his mastery of the English language. When he addressed me quite courteously I soon brought the case of the cockatoos into the conversation, and he immediately became extremely interested. When I told him that I actually had a document to prove the story he became quite excited. We were only a short way from my lodging, and when I produced the document his reaction was startling. Metaphorically, he fell on his knees. I realized that to have a gift accepted by the emperor, who was then a divine being, was an extraordinary honor. He at once asked me what he could do for me.

I explained my predicament, for by this time I knew that my only hope of getting out of the country was by way of a northward route. To the southward the war had fanned out in all directions, and it would have been impossible to get back to our ship. To the northward there were no hostilities, and if I could get across Manchukuo to the Siberian border I would then be able to board the Trans-Siberian Railway. This would involve a journey of many hundreds of miles, but with the help of the Japanese military I would be able to do it. The young officer at once took me to his superior, produced the document again, and with very little ado the necessary passes were prepared and I was quickly headed northward, first to Tientsin, then up to the Great Wall, and eventually on more troop trains across the great plains of Manchukuo.

I stopped in Harbin, the capital of Japanese-occupied Manchukuo, and there for the first time I saw some of the tragic results of the Bolshevik revolution. I stayed in a cheap hotel filled with Japanese officers, and in the dance hall that night I saw a number of very beautiful White Russian women serving as dance partners, and more, for the Japanese officers. These were White Russian girls who had fled the revolution and found that their only possible way to make a living was by prostitution. They were all elegant young women, and they obviously came from well-educated families. But their situation was indeed tragic. I befriended one of these lovely young creatures, whose name I have forgotten, and she told me her fate. She explained, in good French, that she had only one formal dress, which she wore during the evening when she was able to earn a small livelihood, and the rest of the time she remained in her lodgings. It was heartrending to learn of these unfortunate young people, but perhaps they were better off than their male counterparts, some of whom were reduced to pulling rickshaws in the streets, while the more fortunate ones were able to obtain jobs as busboys or elevator operators.

Before reaching the border I took the advice of other travelers in the Far East and took on supplies, such as my limited budget could afford, including a huge loaf of black bread and a very large, greasy sausage, a teapot, and a supply of tea, as I was told the samovars at Russian railroad stations could always supply hot water. This I found to be true. Eventually I reached the border at the little Manchurian town of Chita, and across the border was Manchuli on the Siberian side. Fortunately, a train was due that same day, and I found I had enough money to pay for a fourth-, or "hard-," class fare. This consisted of a bunk covered with straw in a type of cattle car, but at least I was on my way at last.

It was not the most comfortable way to travel, but I had been through too many discomforts by this time to be concerned with that. It was now well on into September, and the Russian winter was approaching. We did encounter some snowstorms. We passed through many wastelands of dwarf birch and fir for hundreds of miles without any signs of human habitation. When we did reach any kind of settlement the people were obviously living under very primitive conditions. Some of them had bundles of straw tied around their legs rather than woolen socks. We passed around Lake Baikal and eventually came to many settlements that were developing rapidly to exploit lumber and mineral resources. Sometimes we passed cattle cars loaded with woebegone-looking people heading for work projects. Obviously these were undesirables, and they certainly looked as if they were doomed, judging by their despairing expressions. Eventually we reached Moscow and I was transferred to another train, continuing on through Warsaw, and eventually reached Hook of Holland and thus to Harwich and home just six years after I had sailed.

By this time I was almost emaciated, having lived on bread and sausage and tea for twenty-two days, with the bread becoming harder every day, the sausage greasier and more tasteless. We were often sidetracked, as the Siberian railroad was then single-tracked, and we would very often wait on a spur for several days while Soviet troops went by. Obviously they were concerned about activities across the border and were reinforcing all of the military installations in that part of the Far East.

I arrived home with just a few shillings in my pocket and weighing 123 pounds. I also had a number of fellow passengers that had emerged from the straw to attack me on the way and was in desperate need of a hot bath. After the warm greetings from my family I was heading upstairs when I heard my mother remark, "He hasn't changed one bit."

Would I have been better off to have remained in that London office? I asked myself, as I reviewed the last six years in retrospect. *Never*, I responded. *I do not have a single regret.* Although I was financially drained, I was rich beyond measure in unforgettable experiences, and as I discovered later, I had seen a world that would never be seen again. Mr. Hilton and his associates had not yet smothered the more attractive places in the world with hotels, hamburgers and Kentucky fried chicken were not being mass-produced in almost every nation, and the beautiful unspoiled islands scattered widely in the vast reaches of the oceans had not yet succumbed to mass international airline transport. Travel could still be an adventure, as I had learned so effectively. And how else could I have established so many close, lasting friendships? Cruising in a small boat is a sure way to create a strong, permanent bond among shipmates; the sea has a way of cementing such bonds. And the sea itself, once an implacable, treacherous enemy, was now a friend, and in a sense, I belonged to her.

7

Marriage and a War

I did not stay in Britain very long. I already realized that my future lay in the United States rather than in Britain, and I had received a tentative offer from a New York publishing house to write a book covering my sailing experiences. So in December 1937 I returned to the United States, making my first formal entry. Again luck was on my side. An old shipmate, Rufus Smith, who had been with me when we sailed *Marit* down from Newfoundland to New York, wanted me to house-sit for him in Bayside, Long Island, so I had an excellent work place for my writing.

The American Yacht Club in Rye had heard of my return and was interested in hearing my narration of the experiences I had undergone during my cruise of the past three years. I was invited to give a talk on New Year's Eve at the Club. It was while I was there that a voice came out of the past. Betty Wellington, whom I had met literally in the middle of Long Island Sound when teaching sailing at the American Yacht Club, had gone back to Bennington College, and since her roommate was the daughter of the commodore, Betty had been able to keep up with my whereabouts. She had received a Christmas card from her roommate informing her that I was to be speaking at the American Yacht Club on New Year's Eve, with the addition at the bottom of a wish for good luck. Shortly before I stood up to give my talk I was told I had

Leigh Creek, England, at low tide, where I spent much of my early life and where the first adventure began.

The *Uldra*, in Long Island Sound.

Pinta aground on Cape Hatteras. This was the first time I set foot on the North American continent.

Uldra entering Long Island Sound, New York.

The schooner *Marit*, still encrusted with sea ice, sailing out of Cabot Strait.

With the two Fahnestock brothers, Sheridan (center and Bruce (right).

Waved albatrosses, Hood Island, Galápagos.

Waterfront beauty, Tahiti.

Dancing girl, Samoa Islands.

Santa Cruz Island villagers, Solomon Islands.

Director sailing into the lagoon at Bora-Bora Island.

Vintas in the Sulu Sea, Philippines.

Two DUKWs entering the sea in a heavy surf. Due to the low center of gravity, DUKWs are extremely seaworthy. With both wheels and propeller engaged, the operator has control over the vehicle at all times, thus avoiding broaching.

A DUKW entering the sea from the ramp of an LST (landing ship tank). The tank deck of an LST can accommodate twenty-one combat-laden DUKWs. This means the LST can remain out of range of enemy shellfire instead of having to go all the way in to the beach.

DUKWs offloading a freighter off Okinawa.

Betty, with Dennis Edward (four) and Jennifer (one), 1944.

Sailing in the Great South Bay, Long Island, with Dennis Edward, age six.

Meadowlark, a field sketch by Dennis Puleston.

Red-eyed vireo, a field sketch by Dennis Puleston.

Painting a merganser, thirty-five years ago.

In doing the check on osprey reproductive success, fledgling chicks like this one were often encountered.

M.S. *Lindblad Explorer* entering Paradise Bay, Antarctica, with two crabeater seals in the foreground.

Rough weather conditions for Zodiac operations alongside the ship, Antarctica.

King penguins at South Georgia, Antarctica.

King penguin chicks, South Georgia. Early explorers called them "oakum boys."

Granddaughter Lyda holds a cayman, a member of the alligator family, caught in the Amazon. It will be released shortly.

Leading a group of birdwatchers in the Falkland Islands.

a telephone call. Somewhat puzzled, I went to the phone and heard this attractive female voice introducing herself as the girl I had fished out of the water several years ago.

I was by this time eager for a family of my own. I have always loved children and wanted my own, and consequently, Betty and I were soon seriously considering marriage, although I did not have the kind of career that would particularly impress Betty's parents. They, however, seemed to be in favor of me as a partner for their daughter, and I realized that between Betty and me we could survive somehow. It was then that another voice came out of the past.

Lewis Hirshon, a shipmate with whom I had established a very strong and warm bond when he sailed with us through some of the Pacific islands, had returned to Tahiti and married his Eugenie. They now had children, and he was interested in developing a business in the islands. One thing that was needed down there was a dependable interisland vessel to serve between Tahiti and some of the sister islands, to bring the products to the central market in Tahiti as well as to transport passengers back and forth. There was another future for an interisland vessel with a good, dependable motor, and that was the beginning of a tourist business. He had found such a vessel, a diesel-powered yacht 105 feet long, on the West Coast and somehow managed to track me down.

In early 1939 Lewis reached me by telephone and asked me if I would be willing to come along as navigator, while he shipped up a Tahitian crew. I readily responded, on the one condition, that I could bring Betty as my wife. To this Lewis answered favorably, and so we were hastily married on February 2, 1939, which also happend to be Groundhog Day, and headed west. It must have been a great strain on Betty's mother's abilities to produce a proper trousseau for a girl going to the tropics and then heading for Britain. But nevertheless, she managed to do a splendid job in a very limited time, and so Betty and I set off across the Continent.

We were met by Lew and Eugenie, who was now pregnant again, and soon boarded *Memory*. I must admit my first reaction was one of some apprehension. She was a typical West Coast power yacht of that period. Designed entirely for operating in local waters, she had quite low freeboard, was somewhat narrow, and was obviously going to be very lively at sea. But she did have plenty of space. Lew had already started a cattle ranch in Tahiti and therefore wanted to take along a young brahma bull. A pen was built for Ferdinand on the stern. We also loaded on a piano and about eighty tons of mixed cargo, including cement, barbed wire, and other fencing materials, all stowed in the forward hatch.

The Tahitian crew arrived, very excited at being in California. We had one amusing experience with them: We took them to one of the larger motion picture houses in Los Angeles, and during the course of the program one of them needed to go to the toilet. We showed him where to go, but a little later there was a big hullaballo and we found out what had happened. Entering a large lounge with potted palms around, he was not aware that the urinals were in a separate room. He thought that the palms were the proper things to be watered and proceeded to do so. When an usher caught him committing the act, there was a great fuss. We had to go into detailed explanations to clear the man of getting into considerable trouble, by explaining his innocence. We also had trouble with Tutu, the cook, who became so intoxicated during his convivial encounters with the local Tahitian population that he became completely lost. He was picked up crawling on all fours along the street, and we had to bail him out of jail.

Eventually we sailed, and outside San Francisco Harbor, where we had picked up our cargo, we ran into a very heavy northwester, and the ship rolled alarmingly. To my surprise, I found that without exception all our Tahitians were seasick and completely demoralized by the cold. Lewis, Betty, and I were left to handle the ship as best we could for the first few days. We had trouble with leaking hatchcovers, with shifting cargo, and particularly with the condition of poor Ferdinand the bull. We were finally able to solve his situation, as he staggered back and forth in his pen, by padding him in with bales of hay, so that he was more or less secured down in one position. This was better than having him slide back and forth and injure himself. The ship rolled violently; we even stove in one of the boats we carried in davits. It was not until five days out, when we were out of the storm, that the first Tahitian crewman emerged on deck. In the meantime, poor pregnant Eugenie had been thrown out of her bunk and for a while we had the terrifying thought of having to perform some midwifery, but fortunately everything held in place, so that did not add to our problems.

We ran into good weather as we cruised into the trade-wind belt, but at times we were without movement, since Oscar, the engineer, was having trouble with the twin engines. Eventually it appeared that one of them needed to be cannibalized to keep the other one going. Oscar had served on the *Memory* for a number of years, but he was not the kind of material that should have

been going to sea. He was not only seasick, he was terrified, and we had great problems in maintaining his morale throughout the rest of the voyage. It developed that
Edgar, a young Tahitian boy, had a natural instinct for
engines and was much more helpful than Oscar. Without
Edgar we wondered whether we would still be drifting
around in the mid-Pacific.

Again, thanks to Oscar, we ran out of water. This
was a serious situation: we had fourteen people and a
bull that required a good deal of water on board. Oscar
had neglected to fill up the forward tanks, and so when
we came to need the reserve supply we found the tanks
were empty. We had plenty of wine, we also had canned
goods with liquids, so we were not likely to die of thirst,
but these were of no use to poor Ferdinand. Fortunately,
however, we ran into a series of tropical rainstorms, and
by spreading out canvas and catching all the water we
could, we had enough to keep the bull going until we
reached the Marquesas.

These islands were very little different from when I
had visited them several years before: still beautiful, still
rarely visited, still greatly underpopulated. Here we were
able to fill our tanks with water by going ashore with
barrels to one of the many mountain streams, so we could
then proceed on our way. We also stopped at Makatea
Island, where phosphates were being mined, and from
there we headed on for Papeete, where we received a
great reception.

Tahiti had not changed perceptibly since I was there
four years ago. Mass tourism and its attendant commer-
cialism were yet to come. There was no airport, and visits
by international shipping were still infrequent. The waterfront girls were present, but they seemed to be a different group; at least I didn't spot any familiar faces. I

presumed the girls I had known were now settled down into domesticity. Several men I knew from the past teased me for bringing my American bride here. "Why," they said, "this is a case of shipping coals to Newcastle!" Perhaps so, but Betty and I were supremely happy.

We spent several months in Tahiti and the neighboring islands. We went on *Memory*'s first runs to the Islands under the Wind (Les Îles sous le Vent), thus initiating her into her interisland career. Surely no honeymoon could have been more delightful than ours. Some of the time we stayed at Lew Hirshon's home out in Pirae; sometimes we just wandered around the island, stopping off at little villages for the night. Sometimes we went to Mooréa and some of the other islands. It was here that we met Sterling Hayden, who was then mate on Irving Johnson's *Yankee*, a man whom I came to know better later on in his career. At that time Sterling, a fine sailor and navigator, had not yet become a film star.

Since by this time I realized that my future lay in the United States, rather than in Britain, it was necessary for me to go to England to initiate procedures for an immigration visa. At the end of this idyllic period for Betty and me in the South Pacific, the Messageries Maritimes ship arrived from the Orient and picked us up, and we headed eastward through the Marquesas to the Panama Canal, through several French islands in the Caribbean, and eventually to Marseilles. I, of course, wanted to reach England for other reasons besides a visa, and that was for my parents to meet their new daughter-in-law.

It was now the summer of 1939, and there was talk of argument about the Baltic port of Danzig. Hitler was ranting on the podium, though all this seemed of very little concern for Britain. But the storm clouds were definitely gathering, as relationships became more tense. Eventually the British woke to the fact that they might come under aerial attack, as Poland had been, so a large-scale evacuation of children from the more vulnerable areas was organized.

I received my immigration visa several days before war broke out, and Betty and I were on our way back to the States when we learned that Britain and Germany were at war. Thus the ship was blacked out and we zig-zagged the rest of the way across the Atlantic. It was just a stroke of luck that we had not sailed on the *Athenia*. We had been offered a berth on her and we would have been in steerage, since we were traveling the cheapest way possible. It was in steerage that most of the passengers were lost when she was torpedoed by a German U-boat shortly after leaving Scotland.

Betty and I reached New York, and I settled down to developing a career in painting. This was a very modest but lucrative form of art, decorating coasters, cigarette boxes, ashtrays, and other luxury items with game birds and waterfowl for the sporting goods trade. It was routine work, but I became very quick at it and to my surprise was making as much as sixty dollars a day, which seemed at that time like a small fortune. In addition to this bread-and-butter type of work, I had time to start a collection of watercolor paintings on fifteen-by-twenty-inch board of the birds of Long Island in their natural habitats, using quick field sketches and stuffed museum specimens as my models. This developed into a lasting hobby, in which I could indulge whenever I was home and had the time. It has lasted to this day and is perhaps one way in which I can express my sentiments toward birds, and as mentioned at the beginning of this story, my first and lasting love affair has been with them.

They are the most perfect embodiment of all that is beautiful and alive in nature, they are sinless, and their lives are without blemish. It is these qualities that endear them to so many of us.

We moved to Brookhaven, near Betty's parents' home on the south shore of Long Island, and in 1940 our first son, Dennis Edward, was born, to our great joy. By this time I was beginning to feel more and more like a U.S. citizen, and by early 1942 I was naturalized and was thus officially one of them. It was this that enabled me to accomplish what I did during World War II.

8

Interlude with a DUKW

The Japanese attack on Pearl Harbor on December 7, 1941, was to affect the lives of almost every living soul in the United States. Its major effect on me began a few months after that "day of infamy." Although on my way to attaining U.S. citizenship, I was still an alien, so was obliged to wait for the day when I could enlist in the military effort. The Offshore Patrol, operated by the U.S. Coast Guard, appealed to me; many of my sailing friends were now manning converted yachts on submarine watch off our coasts, and I felt that this would be my logical assignment as soon as I was naturalized.

But, once again, past contacts were to result in radical changes in my future. A phone call brought the surprising invitation: would I come immediately to work on the design of military craft for Sparkman & Stephens? S & S, as the firm is known throughout the yachting community, had been for many years one of the leading yacht designers and brokers in the United States, but World War II had brought about abrupt changes in their work. They were now involved in the design of various types of craft for the armed forces. Staff was being expanded, and the Stephens brothers, Rod and Olin, recalled meeting me at Cruising Club of America meetings and knew of my interest in boat design and my early training in that field. I indicated to them that I still needed a few more months before I would be naturalized, but that I had been told that I could do unclassified work until that time. So I went to work at the drafting table at the S & S offices in New York City. My first assignment was some detailed deck layouts for the 110-foot submarine chaser.

I cannot say I was too excited by this kind of work, but at least I was contributing to the war effort, albeit in a very small way. Very soon an exciting development arose that would afford me a radical change in my work. The DUKW was primarily the brainchild of ingenious Yankee Dr. Vannevar Bush, who was head of the Office of Scientific Research and Development (OSRD), the wartime agency that coordinated all U.S. military scientific work. Dr. Bush was a farseeing man; he was quick to realize that as the Allies went on the offensive we would need to land enormous masses of men and materials across many of the coastlines of the world. Here was Hitler's *Festung Europa*, with most of the European coastlines defended by his forces or those of his Italian ally, while the Japanese held many of the islands in the South Pacific and also in Indonesia and other parts of the Far East. All the coastlines would be heavily defended, and we would have the challenging task of establishing footholds and then maintaining and expanding them, by means of a constant flow of men and weapons and other supplies.

It was obvious that we would not have the use of conventional port facilities in order to make our landings. It therefore would be necessary to transport all these men and supplies across open beaches, sometimes across coral reefs, and very often in conditions of high surf. How best to perform this task? To concentrate great bodies of men at the waterside to manhandle supplies and load them

135

into land vehicles would certainly be a first-class mistake. First, this would be a misuse of our troops; second, they would be concentrated on the open shoreline, the most vulnerable point.

Dr. Bush reasoned that we must have some kind of an amphibian that would operate both as a seaborne vessel and also as a land-based vehicle. There were basically two choices. One would be a "ground-up" design, which would involve many months at the drawing board and then the establishment of an assembly line to produce this device. The other choice, although something of a compromise, would be a "conversion" design—in other words, to convert an existing piece of equipment and "amphibianize" it. There was one obvious candidate for this that would enable us to go into production quite rapidly. The two-and-one-half-ton six-by-six army truck, with the code designation CCKW,* was then in high production. Would it not be possible, Dr. Bush reasoned, for an amphibious body to be wrapped around the basic chassis and engine with the addition of the necessary marine components? Preliminary discussions with the engineers at the Yellow Truck and Coach Division of General Motors indicated their enthusiasm for the plan. The DUKW was born.

So it was up to S & S to design a watertight amphibious hull that would protect the personnel and cargo, would be able to be loaded from a ship at sea, and could ferry its load to the shore and, without stopping, proceed to the front lines or wherever it was needed most. A hull,

*The General Motors symbols should be explained: C: 1941; C: conventional; K: front-wheel drive; and W: two rear-driving axles. D: 1942; U: utility (amphibious); K: front-wheel drive; and W: two rear-driving axles. It is perhaps fortunate that the DUKW was not designed in 1944, or a vulgar word would have resulted.

propeller, and driveshaft were developed, a rudder was attached to the steering cables at the post of the steering wheel, bilge pumps were added, and the engine was located under a watertight forward deck. Cooling air was drawn forward by a fan on the engine through an airspace behind the driver's cab, where surf would not be likely to drown out the engine. Behind the airspace was an adequate cargo space, which would accommodate as many as thirty men or even a 105-millimeter howitzer or several tons of ammunition or other supplies. The driveshafts to the six wheels were all housed in watertight sleeves. Bilge pumps operated off the main driveshaft. At the rear of the DUKW was a winch that could be used to operate an A-frame to unload another DUKW or to winch oneself when mired down in soft sand or mud.

A pilot model was quickly constructed at Pontiac, Michigan, and a local duck pond served to float the first DUKW. She floated easily, swimming across the pond, the wheels were engaged on the far side, and she climbed out very happily. So we were on our way. Very soon we had five more constructed and we began testing them on Cape Cod. In the meantime, the military showed no interest whatsoever in the new ungainly-looking but very serviceable device. We tried to get high brass out of the Pentagon to see its performance, but this was not possible. They were not interested in new devices. They told Dr. Bush they had too many of them as it was. So the few DUKWs we had, initiated by Dr. Bush himself, were not receiving any support at all from the military. We began staging demonstrations at the Fifth Engineer Special Brigade Headquarters at Camp Edwards on Cape Cod and by using ammunition boxes loaded with sand began calculating rates of discharge per DUKW, coming up with some very impressive figures.

This was now the wintertime, and the weather was bad. Very often DUKWs had to operate under conditions of heavy surf, but we found them extremely seaworthy, due largely to the very low center of gravity and low profile. Another remarkable feature of the DUKW is that it is able to negotiate quite large breakers, due to the fact that at all times there is control over the vessel, whereas even the best-handled surf boat, once its keel hits the ground in the trough of a wave, is more or less helpless. With both the propeller and wheels engaged, the DUKW is afloat one moment, its direction controlled by its rudder; the next moment it is land-borne in the trough of a wave and is controlled by the steering wheel and by the turning of its front wheels. Thus it is able to maintain a course at right angles to the breakers at all times and thus avoids being broached. We were able to handle these devices in quite heavy surf and on one occasion were able to conduct a rescue, which brought much-needed attention to the DUKW's abilities.

It happened this way: One night the Coast Guard requested the aid of one of the DUKWs to rescue the crew of a yacht that had been performing offshore patrol duty along the coast but had been forced ashore on Peaked Hill Bar by storm conditions. Since there were intervening sandbars it was difficult for one of the Coast Guard's surf boats to perform the rescue, whereas for the DUKW it was a simple matter to engage the wheels and the propeller, go into the surf, cross the sandbars, pick up the personnel on board, and bring them ashore. By morning the yacht was gone, and it was never seen again.

Somehow, word of this reached the Joint Chiefs of Staff, and at a meeting in Washington a few days later with President Roosevelt present, Colonel Knox, the secretary of the navy, and Henry Stimson, secretary of the army, engaged in a little banter, Stimson reminding Knox that one of his trucks had gone to sea and rescued a naval vessel. This brought a chuckle to an otherwise serious meeting, and the question arose: what was this device? At last the Pentagon was aroused out of its armchairs, and the next we knew, twenty-five more DUKWs were being prepared on the assembly line at the General Motors plant.

In the early days of my involvement with the DUKW, I came to know very well two individuals who played important roles in the development and operation of amphibians. They were two intensely interesting characters, very dissimilar in their backgrounds. The first was Palmer Putman, an eccentric but brilliant thinker, a man who believed in his own importance and feared no man, however many stars he carried on his lapels. He was a brilliant innovator and was at ease talking at the very highest echelons. I remember hearing him on the phone once demanding a Liberty ship, a dirigible, and six bottles of his favorite hair tonic, all in the same breath. The fact that all three items were forthcoming indicates the power of his personality. He was a truly fascinating man, and it was disappointing to me that our paths diverged later on in the DUKW history as he became involved in other military equipment and techniques.

The other man was Rod Stephens, brother of Olin, both of them highly renowned in yachting circles. Rod was bursting with energy and enthusiasm, tireless, and dedicated. It was again my misfortune to have so little time with him, as he spent more time back at the office, involved in improvement in design of some of the ancillary equipment on DUKWs, such items as the development of a tire pressure control system and other engineering developments that were invaluable to bring out the perfect super-DUKW toward the end of the war. Rod was an outstanding companion, and a man I will never forget.

I was sent down to Fort Story, Virginia, to assist in training operations, and a demonstration was staged to show how DUKWs could outperform any other means of transportation in getting military supplies ashore on an open beach. It was a comparative demonstration, with LCVPs, which are small ramped landing craft, being used to show how it would be done by means of opening the ramp, forming a line of personnel waist-deep in the wintry surf handing ammunition boxes from one to the next up the beach, then loading the boxes into land trucks and driving them off to a simulated dump area within the dunes. This involved a large number of men standing in the surf. I felt sorry for them, working under such conditions.

In the meantime, four DUKWs went out to the Liberty ship offshore, accepted their loads of cargo with just two men in each DUKW, swam across the intervening deep water, climbed out through the breakers onto the beach, and proceeded directly to the dump without a single pause. It was a very stirring demonstration, and from then on the DUKWs had no problems in terms of acceptance. Admiral Hewitt, commander of the Mediterranean Fleet, immediately demanded 25,000 DUKWs, which of course was an impossibility. Representatives of the other theaters of operations also put in their bids.

So General Motors was then in full production of DUKWs, and the next task for me was to set up training centers where we could teach men how to operate these specialized craft, how to maintain them, and how to get the most out of them. Following the fairly small center at Fort Story, Virginia, I was sent down to Charleston,

South Carolina, to set up a training center on the Isle of Palms, one of the islands fronting the sea. Here we established a large DUKW training school, with the full support of the military. We began organizing DUKW companies. These were made up largely of personnel from port battalions, out of the Transportation Corps. The enlisted men of these companies were all Negroes, with white officers. Many of these men had never seen the sea before, but for them the opportunity to operate their own vehicles, instead of merely being stevedores working in the holds of ships, was a big step forward. They took great pride in their vehicles; they were allowed to give them their own chosen names. Each company was assigned twenty-one DUKWs, with a mobile machine shop to go along with them. We began getting into high production in training DUKW companies.

From there it was a quick step to send them overseas. Some went to North Africa, and some went to the South Pacific. I was now working for OSRD and was sent along in the early days to the Ellice Islands in the South Pacific, where we were beginning to take the offensive. I found ready acceptance, although it was always an uphill battle to insist on proper maintenance for these craft. The constant exposure to salt water was a problem; they did require frequent lubrication of all moving parts, such as the strut-bearing and the various universal joints under the vehicle. In order to do this DUKW companies needed to have their personnel trained in first-echelon maintenance. Without this, in the hands of untrained operators, the vehicles were very quickly deadlined, as we saw at Iwo Jima and in some of the other later Pacific campaigns.

The trained army DUKW companies did extremely well; the troops who operated them did a splendid job. At

Iwo Jima they managed to keep going when all of the Marine Corps DUKWs had been deadlined after the third day, operating under very bad conditions. Following the Ellice Islands operation, I learned that I was required by OSRD to continue traveling westward around the world. Although I wore a uniform, I had no insignia of rank. I found this to be a great advantage. One is inclined in dealing with the military to develop certain attitudes toward certain ranks, whereas having no rank, I was able to argue with generals and at the same time maintain friendly relations with the enlisted men. Many times I had frank discussions with them, particularly with some of the splendid staff sergeants who were responsible for DUKW maintenance and repair. I transmitted their important recommendations back to the engineers at General Motors, so that the necessary modifications could be incorporated into the DUKWs that were yet to come off the assembly line.

During my travels through the South Pacific theater of operations, several times I encountered Capt. Irving Johnson, whom I had met in the islands while sailing in *Director*. We heard of many instances during the war of people being given the wrong assignment, like square pegs in round holes. But in Irving's case, here was a man ideally suited for the task he was given. He was in command of the converted power yacht, *Sumner*, and his job was to survey and chart the anchorages to be used by our military vessels.

Before the war, Irving and his wife, Exy, had circumnavigated the world seven times in their schooner *Yankee*, taking as crew groups of paying passengers, mostly college students. Each cruise lasted a year, and crew members were required to stand regular watches and participate in running the ship in every way. Irving was a strict disciplinarian and an outstandingly competent skipper, and every crew member gained a lasting experience from sailing with him. He was a physical fitness buff and would sometimes swarm up a pole and do one-arm handstands from the top. He had sailed on every type of sailing vessels, including the square-rigger *Peking*, rounding Cape Horn under stormy conditions. Irving was a remarkable man, and it was gratifying to see him serving the war effort in a way that made the best possible use of his experience and abilities.

I arrived in the Solomon Islands while the last of the Japanese troops were being driven off Guadalcanal. This had been a particularly bloody campaign, with casualties high on both sides. Jungle fighting was a new experience for our marines, but they adapted well to the very difficult conditions, which included malaria, heat, and frequent shortages of supplies. At that time, the European theater was at the top of the priorities list, and the South Pacific was desperately in need of both men and matériel.

I wondered how successful our campaigns in this theater would have been without the magnificent contribution made by the handful of men known as coast watchers. Before the war, these men were either plantation managers or British and Australian government administrators. When the Japanese moved in, they disappeared into the jungle rather than surrender. From their hiding places they were able to monitor Japanese troop activities, and by means of radios supplied by U.S. submarines they could transmit this kind of important information to our forces. Many times prior to takeoff Japanese planes were lined up on their runways, where they could be destroyed by the U.S. Army Air Corps while they were most vulnerable. The Japanese had committed a fateful error in mistreating and even enslaving the native people, who were eager to support the coast-watching activities and could act as spies around the Japanese bases without being suspect. I had the privilege of meeting some of these coast watchers and hearing of their heroic, lonely exploits and wish they could receive the full recognition they deserve for the vital roles they played in the fighting in the Solomons–New Guinea area.

From the Solomons I was sent to Douglas MacArthur's headquarters at Brisbane, Australia. Here I was shocked to find that an adverse report on DUKWs had come from New Guinea and that the DUKW companies were being used entirely for land transportation. Something must be seriously wrong. I requested authorization to go to Milne Bay and Finschaven, where these DUKWs had been grounded, to find out what had happened. The report indicated that they were unseaworthy, which was of course utterly ridiculous.

When I reached Milne Bay I found that several of our trained companies from the Charleston school were already there. They were in a great state of frustration, having to be used only for land operations. In making inquiries, I found the root of this situation. It appeared that before the arrival of the trained companies several DUKWs without trained crews had been sent to the New Guinea theater and put in the hands of a most unimaginative port officer, with the request that they be tested out for water operations. Without reading any of the directions about operation and maintenance of DUKWs, he simply ordered some of his men to drive them into the water, to see how they performed. These DUKWs had been shipped on the deck of a Liberty ship and, as was often the case, their bilge plugs had been left open in order to get rid of any rain and sea that had collected in the hulls.

When the DUKWs were offloaded on land and then driven into the water, naturally the water poured through the bilge drains and they very quickly submerged. Without trying to find the reason for this, the officer responsible sent back a report: the DUKWs were "unseaworthy" and should not be used for water transportation. Thus the problem had arisen. I, of course, was obliged to go over the head of the port officer and contact his superior. When I explained the situation, he readily agreed that we should stage a demonstration by having our trained DUKW companies discharge some of the many vessels waiting to be unloaded. The result was spectacular; the companies were able to discharge the ships at rates that had been unheard of in New Guinea up to that time.

From then on there were no more major problems with DUKWs in the southwest Pacific. They were in great demand everywhere, not only for discharging ships during the garrison phase of an operation, but also during the combat phase, when they were frequently under fire. Due to their low profile they managed to survive very handily. Some of them were even equipped with rocket launchers, as was the case in the New Britain campaign. Although the southwest Pacific theater was not given as high a priority in matériel during the early days of the war, many DUKW companies were now arriving. Since they were self-sufficient, they were able to follow the island hopping and the operations along the north coast of New Guinea, Biak, Manus, and many of the other large islands.

It was painful for me, as it was for many other millions, to be away from family during the war, wondering if we would ever be reunited with them. I am sure that almost everyone had pangs of homesickness, which were only relieved by the intensity of our lives while engaged in the business of war. I found that writing to Betty as frequently as possible was a great release for me, although I could say very little in my letters about what I was doing or where I was. I mostly rambled on about the family I loved and my hopes for the future of our children. As for mail from home, this came very sporadically; sometimes I would not receive mail for months at a time, as I was moving fairly constantly, and in spite of the admirable system the army used in doing its best to get mail to its rightful recipients, it was extremely difficult to keep track of the millions of us scattered in so many remote parts of the globe. I will never criticize their efforts in bringing us mail, whenever possible, sometimes under the most difficult and primitive conditions.

Another release I found during the war was poring through two books I had brought with me. They told me of another world that had nothing to do with war. One was *Wind in the Willows*. This had always been one of my favorites. It was just a delight to dip into this charming story and revel in the antics of the little animals who were its heroes. The other book was Thoreau's *Walden*, a book of entirely different quality, but one, again, that brought me close to the beauties and joys of nature, when there was so little of it we had time for close at hand. I did, however, regret the lack of any good bird books for the areas I was covering. In places like the Solomons and New Guinea, the bird life was incredibly rich and spectacular in its diversity, and I longed to be able to put names to the many species I saw. It is a rather odd habit we bird lovers have of wanting to put a name on every species we encounter, and if we are unable to do so, we have a sense of frustration. After all, birds are just as beautiful whether one can attach a tag to them or not.

I spent Christmas Day in the Milne Bay area, and there was great excitement when it was announced to the troops that we were to have a motion picture as a special treat. Everyone assembled in front of a large homemade screen and the film started, but much to our disgust we found that it had been prepared by the Medical Corps, describing how to best avoid venereal disease. One can well imagine the catcalls and the cries of outrage by the assembled troops.

Shortly after this I received orders to proceed to the China-Burma-India theater and report to Mountbatten's command. So I flew back to Brisbane, and from there I had to cross Australia to Perth, from where I could be flown up to Ceylon and eventually to New Delhi. It was a strange trip; there were four of us that left Perth in an old PBY, or Catalina flying boat, which does about 120 miles an hour. She was loaded up with many extra tanks of fuel, and we actually spent twenty-eight hours in the air. We made slow progess across the Indian Ocean, eventually landing on the west coast of Ceylon.

When I reached India and reported to Mountbatten's headquarters, I was assigned a billet in a palace belonging to the maharaja of Bikaner, an extremely opulent building, but regrettably, the ladies of the harem had already been moved out. It was a striking change from the primitive quarters I had been accustomed to throughout the Solomons and New Guinea, but at the same time, I could not help sympathizing with the many wives and concubines housed in this palace. There was only one means of access to the ground floor, the ladies were all kept on an upper floor, and there was a sentry box at the foot of the staircase so that no one could enter or leave without a check from the sentry. The quarters upstairs were lavishly Victorian: big brass bathtub fittings and all the luxuries, but unfortunately the only decorations on the walls were photographs of the maharaja and some of his pals after their various hunting trips. These depicted the slaughter of large numbers of tigers, leopards, and other game animals, and the hunters were all rigidly posed behind their trophies. I am sure the ladies could derive little entertainment from these pictures. As far as their access to the out of doors was concered, they had to peer through heavy carved stone windows. The apertures were in the form of filigreed designs, and very little natural light entered the rooms upstairs.

I was too busy myself to be concerned with the misfortunes of these ladies, as I was immediately involved in the planning of future campaigns in the China-Burma-India theater requiring the use of DUKWs. We set up a big training center in Juhu on the outskirts of Bombay, and we began training British troops in DUKW operation. I found them extremely dedicated men in spite of the comparatively poor pay that British troops received. They had much higher morale and greater interest in their assignments than most U.S. troops. They were even held responsible for a missing tool or other piece of equipment on their vehicles; this cost was deducted from their pay. This is in striking contrast to the American troops and the haphazard way in which they lost and mislaid tools and other equipment and in the very poor sense of property they had toward what was needed.

The British soldier will cheerfully survive on short or inferior rations, but he must have his cup of tea, or his morale will suffer. Someone at our training center invented an ingenious device for heating water from the DUKW engine's exhaust manifold; it was quickly copied for all the British DUKWs, and so morale stayed high, even under combat conditions.

The Japanese were using several of the rivers to supply their troops fighting in the interior of Burma. It was Mountbatten's plan to cut off these supply routes by taking the mouths of some of these rivers. Landings were made along the Burma coast quite close to the border with India, and it was here at the Naf River where we made an amphibious landing that a shell from across the river landed close and I was knocked out with a damaged spine. I recall coming to lying in the bed of a truck as we headed toward a medical station nearby. I was in great pain, because several vertebrae had been damaged, there was a dent in my skull, and when I was finally placed in a hospital bed I realized that one of my problems was an inability to urinate. To describe this as a major discomfort is a masterpiece of understatement. I was so wretched I was ready to welcome death.

Help, however, was at hand from a most unlikely source. At that time British medical staff was so scarce in the area that Italian prisoners of war taken in the North African campaigns had been enlisted as hospital aides. They were a sinister-looking lot, small, dark, unshaven men, many of them bearing scars around their faces from knife fights, but they were certainly among the gentlest nurses I have ever come across.

I managed by sign language to indicate my problem, and these men became greatly concerned and took it as a personal challenge to remedy the situation. They went off and huddled in a corner, talking excitedly, with much arm waving, and eventually one of them obviously came to a solution, and all of the others gave a cheer and he was acclaimed the hero of the day. They managed to ease me to the edge of the bed, with my legs hanging down, and soon one of them arrived with a large washbowl full of warm water. They immersed my feet in the bowl, and this had the desired effect. The relief was indescribable. The joy and pride of these Italian nurses was a delight to witness. They were jumping up and down with joy, slapping each other on the back, and from then on I was their prize exhibit. They had literally saved my life, or so they believed. Perhaps they did.

At any rate, from then on I was in much greater comfort, although for a long time I had a very stiff back and walked with some difficulty. X-ray equipment was unknown in that part of the world, and it was many months before I was able to find that a number of vertebrae had been damaged and that my lumbar spine was now seated on the edge of the sacrum. Should it have slipped off, I would have been paralyzed from the waist down, but at that time I was not aware of this situation. A brief announcement reached Betty from the Pentagon, but the details were almost nonexistent. She was merely told that I was seriously injured; the outcome was not known. It says much for her fortitude that she kept on with her normal responsibilities, taking care of our small son and Jennifer, our daughter, who had been born during the early part of the war. I had been in the hospital about ten days when I received orders to proceed to the Mediterranean campaign and from there to Britain to prepare for the landings on Normandy beaches.

On the basis of these orders, I was able to leave the hospital and proceed on my way, stopping off in North Africa, where I was able to give some assistance to the DUKW training school there, eventually arriving in Britain in February 1944. It was then a matter of setting up a DUKW school to prepare many U.S. DUKW companies for landings on the Normandy coast, planned for the following June. We had a suitable area assigned to us in South Wales near Swansea, and the work began. Freshly organized DUKW companies came in, we trained them, and they were shifted to the south coast one after the other. It was difficult to find time to sleep, as there was so much to be done.

A rather amusing complication arose in DUKW control when confronted with the problem of the British land traffic system, whereby one drives on the left. A question arose: when is a DUKW a seagoing vessel and must stay to starboard and when does she become a landborne vehicle and must stay to the left? This resulted in many near collisions and suchlike complications at the beachhead, because we were training the troops to not only operate the DUKWs at sea, but also to go back into the hinterland and discharge their cargoes at dumps. Besides organizing the DUKW training school I was also in the process of working with Rod Stephens from S & S in drafting a DUKW operator's manual.

London had undergone many changes since my sojourn there many years before. So many parts of the city had been destroyed by German aerial attack, and now the buzz bombs were beginning to arrive. One became used to these after a while, but the first sound of them as they came tearing overhead was somewhat unnerving, because one never knew just where they were going to hit. But the morale of the people was so high that one could not fail to be impressed with the spirit of the Londoners, who had undergone so much, when they were forced to live in Underground stations for months at a time, and yet had remained cheerful and optimistic. I was duly proud of my motherland and wondered how many other nations could have shown such remarkable morale under the terrible bombings through which they had suffered.

As the summer drew near, more and more equipment was piling up in Britain, particularly along the south coast; there was a wry joke to the effect that it was only the barrage balloons that kept the island from sinking into the sea under the weight of all the equipment that was being unloaded. Vast areas were covered with tanks, planes, weapons carriers, and other vehicles of all kinds, including, of course, DUKWs.

By the time the landings came we had some thirty DUKW companies available, in addition to the many companies under British command. At least five or six thousand DUKWs were used during the first few days of the Normandy landings. It was an impressive sight to see the way in which they were able to perform their jobs. I never ceased to marvel at the organization that went on under the leadership of Dwight Eisenhower, to my mind one of the great military geniuses. One of his outstanding qualities was his ability to select a competent staff and assign their responsibilities so that his own decisions could be thought through clearly.

The vital decision to launch the invasions was his, and to my mind the man's greatness shines through most clearly in the statement he had prepared in advance of the event that his troops were repulsed, his planes shot down, and his ships sunk. He wrote: "Our landings in the Cherbourg-Havre area have failed to gain a satisfactory foothold and I have withdrawn the troops." Originally he had written: "The troops have been withdrawn." But knowing that he must accept the ultimate reponsibility, he made this noble revision. He continued: "My decision to attack at this time and place was based on the best information available . . . if any blame or fault attaches to the attempt, it is mine alone." Those last words shine out in a dark and perilous time as the greatest tribute that can be made to a great soldier, a great leader, and a great man.

Much had already been written about the landings on June 6, 1944, so it is not necessary to go into any repetition. My own experiences were none too exciting. I did get over there and saw the remarkable way in which all the necessary men and equipment were landed on open and often storm-battered beaches in short order, so that a massive offensive could be launched. Since the weather for the past few days had been stormy, the Germans were so confident there would be no Allied activities that General Rommel was in Berlin celebrating his wife's birthday. The surprise element was a great factor in the intitial landing, and in the establishment of a permanent beachhead the DUKWs played a major part. In *Crusade in Europe*, General Eisenhower's detailed account of the European campaign, he described the DUKW as ". . . one of the most valuable pieces of equipment produced by the United States during the war."

I remember being up in the dunes, somewhat exhausted, and figuratively catching my breath as the landing took place all around at a feverish pace. In the distance were the sounds of battle, but nearer at hand and directly overhead a skylark was singing in ecstasy. I was deeply moved by this one element of sanity in the whole mad business of war. That bird made me realize that someday all this would be over and I could enjoy birds again the way I had always wanted to. I have never forgotten that one small bird and the effect it had upon me.

I was eventually sent back home and had a couple of months in which to enjoy my family and get to know

Dennis and Jennifer, our two children. But then the orders came for me to proceed back to the Pacific. I went to Oahu in the Hawaiian Islands and set up a training center at Waimanalo, on the east coast of Oahu. We built a large dock to serve as the dummy side of a ship, with a crane above, and thus we trained the troops in the proper system for using a spring line to come under the crane and accept the cargo. By this time our campaigns were bringing us ever closer to the Japanese mainland, and it appeared that eventually a landing would have to be made on the island of Honshu. The prospect was terrifying; we had seen how desperately the Japanese had fought almost to the last man in defending their strongholds in the scattered islands all through the Pacific. How much more desperately would they fight when defending their homeland? We were told that even small boys were being armed with bamboo spears, that the bombing of their cities would not cause them to surrender. So we realized that there were many bloody operations ahead of us. In the meantime the Iwo Jima campaign took place, of which much has been written, and later on Okinawa. The latter campaign started off well, with very little opposition, but the Japanese forces were concentrated on the southern end of the island, and from there they fought with the usual desperation. So Okinawa was a long campaign, as compared to Iwo Jima, which, although it resulted in tremendous American casualties, was relatively short-lived.

At Okinawa we were confronted with Japanese kamikaze aerial attacks. It was an impressive sight when one of these small one-man planes came diving in while all the ships at sea and the shore batteries were firing everything they could at it. If one believed in the ultimate glory of dying for one's divine emperor, it was certainly a satisfactory way to sacrifice one's life. It was a great strain on the ships in the anchorage off Okinawa; the vessels carrying freight were desperate to get out of there as quickly as possible. This presented our DUKW operators with a problem. Quite frequently netloads of cargo would come down to them that would be too much for the capacity of the DUKW. There were several incidents where DUKWs were actually sunk by overloads. We called all the DUKW operators together and told them that if they saw a load coming down that was not a sensible size, they were to cast off immediately and refuse to accept it. In one instance a black driver saw this huge netload coming down and realized it was beyond the capacity of his craft, so he immediately released the spring line that was holding him against the side of the ship. At once an officer on the deck began screaming obscenities at him and ordering him to come back and accept the load. The black driver looked at him and said, "And who are you?" "I am the first officer on this ship," came the response, upon which the DUKW driver replied with great dignity, "Well, I am the captain of this here vessel and I don't take no orders from my inferiors." And he refused to take that load. This was the morale of our DUKW drivers right up to the end. They performed admirably.

As the masses of military equipment continued to pile up on Okinawa, from whence the landings on the Japanese mainland were to be launched, we began to receive briefings and a solemn warning that casualties would be extremely heavy, a million being anticipated during the first phase of the landings. This resulted in great tension among all of us. For although we were extremely well equipped, we knew that the Japanese had plenty of fight still left in them.

It was a complete surprise to us when we learned that a fearsome new weapon, the atomic bomb, was dropped on Hiroshima and then a second one on Nagasaki. The Japanese, of course, had no way of knowing that these were the only two bombs available, but this new weapon had the desired effect, and the emperor called for peace terms. There has been much controversy ever since on the ethics of using this incredibly destructive force, with the resultant terrible loss of Japanese lives and lasting injuries, and Pres. Harry Truman has been criticized harshly for making the ultimate decision to use it. But in considering the far greater number of casualties, both American and Japanese, that would have been involved in a conventional assault on the Japanese mainland, one is forced to conclude that this particular use of the atomic bomb actually saved millions of lives, and much further destruction of Japanese cities by normal bombing raids.

We were in our tent in the early evening, listening to the radio, when we heard the announcement that the Japanese emperor was asking for surrender terms. This should have been a most joyous moment, but it quickly became a period of terror. The island went mad; somebody began shooting a rifle, and this very quickly developed into a barrage of ammunition of all kinds and sizes from all directions. All the ships in the harbor began firing in celebration, and the troops on shore did likewise. We had been listening intently to the radio when a bullet cut through the top of the tent and somebody shouted, "To the foxholes!" We dived in, when a sergeant following me gave a yell as a bullet cut through his wrist. That night a number of people died in this wild orgy of celebration, which should never have happened. But it was the only way men had of relieving the tensions. It was a sad commentary that people had to die in the moment when hostilities came to an end.

I did not remain very much longer in Okinawa but headed homeward to a wonderful reunion with my family.

9

Alligators in the Bathtub

As was the case with millions of others, the end of the war began a new stage for me. This was a fitting time to get to know my family, to revel in the atmosphere of peace and euphoria that surrounded us, and for a while I thought little of a new career. I had a five-year-old son and a two-year-old daughter to get to know. I was just back basking in the glories of being a family man with a home in the little hamlet of Brookhaven on the south shore of Long Island, New York. I did have to do something about my back injury, however. This required a major decision. Having X rays taken and discovering that the lumbar spine was now resting on the edge of the sacrum, I had to decide whether I should have a spinal fusion, which would involve taking a piece of bone out of my hip to serve as a peg to render immobile my lower spine. Or was I willing to take a chance on it and try to avoid the dangers of having the lumbar spine slip entirely off the sacrum, which would result in paralysis from the waist down? I decided to take a chance and skip the six months or so that would be required to remain immobile to ascertain whether the fusion would take or not. There was too much going on and too many things I wanted to do. I was quickly brought into a new career.

The OSRD, for whom I had worked during the war years, was required by the government to assemble a series of volumes describing all the scientific projects for the military establishment in which that office had been involved. It was my assignment to write up a detailed technical report on the responsibilities of the division involved with transportation, which included the development and subsequent use of DUKWs throughout the various theaters of war. Fortunately, I was able to do most of this work at home. But having completed this assignment, I found that I was then becoming involved in the work of assembling the research of all the other divisions of OSRD. This required commuting into New York City for two and one-half years. We rented a complete floor in the Empire State Building and under our contract with the Columbia University Division of War Research had a fairly large organization to assemble all this material. We hired editors, illustrators, indexers, and technical writers from many fields to complete this mammoth operation. As the project progressed, we were able to shrink in size until we had a mere handful of people to complete the production of the seventy-two volumes involved, many of which were classified. Toward the end of this project I became the director of the group. In early 1948, it was completed, and the seventy-two volumes were turned over to the Pentagon.

In the meantime, to my utter amazement, I was presented by President Truman with the Freedom Medal for my wartime activities. I am absolutely convinced I am the least deserving recipient of this recognition, since it is the highest civilian award in the United States. I can think of so many others who were more deserving of it than I. Be that as it may, I did receive this significant honor.

Just about the time when the OSRD project was winding down, I was able to step into another position that was developing only twelve miles away from my home. This was the creation of a large research laboratory involved in basic research in the peaceful applications of the recently discovered force of nuclear energy. It was apparent that no single private organization could finance and undertake a project of such magnitude, so it was funded by the newly formed U.S. Atomic Energy Commission and administered by Associated Universities, Inc., a consortium of nine northeastern universities.

Brookhaven National Laboratory was therefore established on Long Island in what had been Camp Upton, a wartime army induction center of thirty-five hundred acres of scrub and pine. The early offices and research facilities were located in old army barracks buildings. Since I was already involved in the preparation of scientific reports and was well known at Columbia University, where the initial plans for the laboratory were being laid, I was enlisted to organize a technical information division at the laboratory. This was just another remarkable instance of the part that luck has played during my lifetime. Here I was, living only a few miles away from this newly formed job, whereas others, scientists and technicians from many different fields, had to be brought into the area. This was then a remote agricultural part of Long Island with little housing and few other amenities.

So starting in early 1948 and for the next twenty-three years, I worked at this splendid laboratory, associating with many of the finest scientists and engineers in the country in a most rewarding field. During my last ten years at Brookhaven, I was able to satisfy some of my urge to travel. As president of the United States, Dwight Eisenhower initiated the Atoms for Peace Program. This was directed toward developing nations who wanted their own atomic energy programs. Whether they needed one or not was another matter; this was one phase of their growing up. Eisenhower wisely decided that it was much better to give them assistance in developing meaningful programs that would be beneficial to them, rather than allowing them to go off on their own and perhaps get into difficulties.

So a program was organized for sending groups of U.S. scientists and engineers to the various countries indicating a desire for a national nuclear energy program and setting up scientific institutes as well as public areas in order to encourage the scientists of the countries to use nuclear energy as a beneficial research tool, and also to convince the general population that they could benefit. We would visit many of the countries under this program, including Pakistan, Thailand, the Netherlands, Taiwan, the Philippines, Ireland, and Indonesia. Part of the institute was a small research reactor, a gamma-irradiation facility, and a technical information center, along with a public area where simple exhibits were displayed. For the latter part of the program we invited the assistance of local university-level students, who received a two-week training period prior to working at these public displays.

This turned out to be a very delightful project, although it involved much hard work and long hours without any relief. I myself enjoyed greatly working with these fine young people as director of the Technical Information Institute. I used several students as assistants and found in every case that this was a rewarding experience, many resulting in lasting friendships. At the end of 1970, however, I reached the mandatory retirement age of sixty-five, since my birthday came on December 30, 1969. I was then free to devote more of my time to other projects and interests, as well as to my own family.

Two more children, Peter and Sally, had been born

to Betty and me in 1946 and 1949. Now we had four children, all born three years apart, and of alternating sexes. It was my privilege to be able to live in a pleasant area and to be able to watch them grow up, with time to pursue my other loves, in ornithology and sailing. It was soon apparent that all four children had a very strong interest in wildlife. Living as we did among Brookhaven's meadows on the banks of a small river, with an extensive salt marsh and the Great South Bay beyond, we had an ideal setup for nurturing such interests.

All of the time the children were growing up we had a succession of pets of many kinds, and as soon as one was rehabilitated along came another. In the neighborhood the Puleston family had a reputation for being a kind of hospital and repository for any orphaned, injured, or lost animal, and these creatures were always accepted, from young minks to several species of hawk, woodcocks, owls, nighthawks, and many small birds. I remember the nighthawk particularly; it had been struck by a car, and although its wing was not broken, it was damaged so the bird was unable to fly for a while. We had it for several weeks during the fall migration, and it chose to roost on a log in our fireplace. We fed it dried flies obtainable at the pet stores, and it seemed to do very well, and much to our relief we were finally able to release it under favorable migratory conditions and watch it heading south on seemingly strong wings.

Another delightful bird we had for several months was a bobwhite quail. He had been struck by a car, and when I picked him up in the middle of the road I thought he was dead, but he recovered and lived with us for all of one winter. Again the fireplace came to good use, and his seed was always placed there. In the following spring he was able to return to the wild, a perfectly healthy bird.

We also had a female kestrel. This bird had been severely damaged, one leg was atrophied, and one wing was so damaged the bird would never fly again. She had been found at the side of the road by a friend, and we took her in. Normally when a bird is that severely damaged, it loses the will to survive and nothing can persuade it to attempt to recover; it will refuse food and if food is forcibly fed, it will reject it. It is just determined to die, but this was not the case for this lovely little falcon. She was determined to live, and in spite of her one wing and one leg, she lived with us for several years before we turned her over to the Quogue Wildlife Refuge. She was an admirable little bird, and I always think of her with much affection and respect.

All four of the children were a great delight to Betty and me. We derived so much pleasure from them and shared so many joys and interests. The second boy, Peter, at a very early age developed what would be a lifelong interest in reptiles and amphibians. One of my early recollections of him occurred when he was about five years of age. I awakened early one morning and heard a quiet sobbing coming from his bedroom. Upon investigating, I found that the large blacksnake that he was caring for and had secreted in his bed for the night was exploring the hole in the floor through which the radiator pipes led to the cellar. The snake was slowly slipping through his hands and disappearing through the hole, and perhaps Peter thought he was losing his friend forever. I dashed outside, descended to the cellar, and grabbed the other end of the snake, much to Peter's relief.

We became enamored of crows; they are such intelligent, if mischievous, birds. Once I brought back a young crow from its nest in the pines at the edge of the salt marsh and we were firmly imprinted on it, so that it regarded us as its parents. It would follow us around everywhere. Even when perfectly able to take care of itself, it still liked to be fed by us simply to reinforce its attachment to us. We gave it hamburger meat, and like any wise crow, when it was satiated and yet had one more helping that it could not consume, it would try to hide it in some suitable area so the bird could come back to it later. Several times when perched on my shoulder it would then proceed to stuff a beakful of hamburger into my ear, its idea of a suitable repository for hiding food.

Later on we had two crows and these crows were so attached to us that even when we were out sailing in the middle of Great South Bay they were able to locate us and land on the decks. One evening, driving home from the laboratory, I had dropped off a friend in another part of Brookhaven and as I was driving along the main road to home I saw a group of ladies looking at a crow that was pecking at their shoes. I stopped and realized that this was one of our two crows. I called to him and he immediately flew over to the car, much to the ladies' astonishment, and he drove home with me.

The onset of spring was always exciting. Even when the children were quite young, it was a pleasure to wander out into the meadows around us and listen at dusk to the remarkable performance of the woodcock as it indulged in its courtship rituals, also the thrill of hearing the first calling of the peeper frogs from the boggy woodlands. The bell-like calls of these tiny frogs is surely the first sign that winter is coming to an end. That along with the first redwing blackbird males establishing territories in the reed beds at the foot of our meadow were signs that better weather was on its way. These rituals have since been repeated with my grandchildren.

In the 1950s, Betty's parents had acquired a piece of property on the east coast of Florida, and we were able to go down there every spring when I took my vacation from my work at the laboratory. There were then still parts of Florida that were truly wilderness, and we had many exciting times with the local wildlife there. Catching baby alligators in the swamps was great sport, and they made interesting pets, the only condition being that we kept them for a year and then we returned them to the habitat from which they had come when we went down the following season. This kept up for several years, and it produced some remarkable experiences for some of our guests. I remember one time a friend who had been indulging in a vigorous game of tennis was desperately in need of a shower. He asked if he might cool off in our bathroom, and of course we agreed. Next thing, we knew he came back with a look of horror on his face, to report that there were alligators in our bathtub, as though they had somehow appeared there by some abstruse means. They, of course, were so much part of our family we thought nothing of it, and when the tub was needed they were simply transferred to the handbasin.

Then there was Daisy the chipmunk. She was brought to us by a neighbor as a barely weaned foundling, and Jennifer immediately claimed her as her own special ward. Daisy spent much of her time nestling inside her foster mother's shirt. At mealtimes Daisy would pop out, inspect the dishes on the table, select an item to her liking, stuff it into her cheek pouches, and then disappear back into the security of Jennifer's teenage bosom. Sometimes Jennifer would head off down the lane to board the school bus, forgetting for the moment that Daisy was with her. Then she would remember, dash back, and

165

hand me the disappointed little animal, who resented eviction from her favorite sanctuary.

Another interesting addition to the family was a young turkey vulture. Betty and I had been canoeing in the Ozarks with friends and had come across this young bird, which was not receiving proper attention, and I had always wanted a vulture. So he came back to Brookhaven, riding in the back of the car, and became very much one of the family. He would sit on my shoulders for hours at a time and accompanied me everywhere, including on car trips. He sat on my shoulder looking out of the driver's window and no doubt causing consternation among other drivers. We christened him Alger because his only voice was a hiss. As he grew older, he became more active and I had to tether him outside. I remember one time he managed to chew through this tether and I found him outside the kitchen door, waiting to be admitted. Our daughter Sally was asked by her high school science teacher to bring Alger to school one day. Apparently, Alger was not too happy about the crowds of people around him, and so he took off and ended up on top of the flagpole in front of the school. This disrupted classes for the entire school. It was not until later in the day, when he flew over to a neighboring rooftop, that someone was able to bring him down and restore him to me. Later on, when I had to do a good deal of traveling for the U.S. Atomic Energy Commission, rather than neglect him I turned him over to the Quogue Wildlife Refuge, where he lived for many years.

We live near the edge of a salt marsh bordered by a strip of deciduous woods. It is an important flyway for birds migrating during the fall season. So I became involved in bird banding, obtaining the necessary federal and state licenses from the U.S. Fish and Wildlife Service and New York State. Using exceptionally fine nets called mist nets, set in narrow lanes cut through bushy areas, I was able to trap, identify, band, record, and release many hundreds of small birds every fall, mostly in the very early mornings, when bird activity is at its peak. The records are all sent to the government's Banding Office in Maryland, where they are computerized, as a program of the U.S. Fish and Wildlife Service. In this way we are learning much about the habits of birds, their migratory routes, age expectancy, population trends, sex ratios, and many other statistics, so it has become a very important activity in ornithological fields. It is rewarding for a bander to be notified when one of the birds he has banded has been recovered by someone else, and there is always the excitement of catching a bird that has not been seen in the area before. Even the more abundant ones are of interest. Being able to handle and examine them closely, seeing how perfect they are, is a very satisfying experience. Here one is able to appreciate details of their plumage one is unable to memorize when they are sneaking through the underbrush.

Many students from the local high school were eager to help in this work, and they came down before they went to class. Early morning is the best time for banding work. The birds have been migrating all night, and in the early morning they settle down to feed, to "refuel their tanks" as it were, before they can relax later on in the day and then continue their migration on the following night. So this became another very satisfying occupation for me. The ornithological possibilities on Long Island are endless. Lying as it does between two of the major life zones, there are many overlaps between birds from the north and birds from the south. In addition to this, there are many varieties of habitat: from the open ocean to the outer beaches, the dunes, the salt marshes, the salt bays, the freshwater ponds, and the deciduous woods and the open fields.

I had endless possibilities for satisfying my interests in nature. I soon became associated with someone who became a very great friend. Arthur Cooley, a teacher at the local high school and a keen biologist, was able to assemble groups of interested students, and we took them on many weekend field trips. Stimulated by my own interests in this field, I found it to be a most rewarding activity to see these young people developing an interest in wildlife. Many of them, following the completion of their education, adopted careers in the biological sciences and have come back to see us many times.

And then there was the sailing. I had some difficulty finding any boat suitable for cruising in the shallow waters in the Great South Bay, but I finally did. She was a thirty-four-foot gaff-rigged yawl with a three-foot draft and a roomy cabin. We called her the *Heron*. We kept her in the river right in our backyard. In her we were able to sail over to the outer barrier beach to fish and clam. Clamming in those days was a delightful pastime; when the waters in the bay were warm enough we would anchor out on the flats in about four feet of water and tread for the clams. You work your feet around in the soft mud, and as soon as you feel one under your foot, you duck down for it and bring it up. Then there is fishing for flounder during the summer and small bluefish known as snappers later on in the season. The blueclaw crab is abundant. The children would frequently go down to the banks of the river with a fish head on a piece of string and, as soon as the line went taut, bring it carefully to the surface and then, with a long-handled dip net, scoop up the crab that was feeding on the bait. We had many delicious meals of these blueclaw crabs.

On the outer dunes the beach plums ripen in September and we make many expeditions to gather them in buckets for producing a delicious jelly with a tangy, distinctive taste. It seems remarkable to me that these juicy-looking plums would grow in such arid habitats on the outer beach, with nothing but sand for their sustenance. But they are a great soruce of nutritious jelly and we still harvest them in the late summer.

Another activity during the late summer and early fall is to conduct hawk counts on the Barrier Beach. We found that this thin strip of dunes fronting the Atlantic on the south shore of Long Island is a major flyway for migrating hawks of several species when the weather conditions are favorable. A northwest wind produces a veritable parade of kestrels, merlins, and lesser numbers of sharp-shinned and Cooper's hawks and ospreys and even a few peregrines. The wind off the dune line gives them a lift as they head southward for their wintering grounds. On suitable days hundreds of birds pass in the course of an hour, providing a thrilling spectacle. At this season the monarch butterflies are also migrating along the shoreline, feeding on the nectar from the bright yellow heads of the seaside goldenrod, making their way southward in great numbers to the subtropical areas where they winter. The females lay eggs on the milkweed plants during their travels, and their progeny, when they reach the adult stage, continue the round-trip on their northward flight in the following spring. It is marvels like these that have enriched our lives and have made Long Island a wonderful place in which to raise a family.

10

The Battle for the Environment

One bird that quickly became a major interest to me was the osprey, or fish hawk. I had never seen one when growing up in Britain. It had been extirpated many years before by the guardians of the Scottish salmon rivers. But on Long Island this was a fairly abundant bird, a magnificent creature that lives entirely on fish. Upon sighting its prey from a great height, it plunges into the water with a huge splash and seizes its victim in its talons. On Long Island in those years, the late forties, there were dozens of nests scattered all along the shorelines. And on Gardiners Island, lying between the two eastern tips of Long Island, there were at that time an estimated three hundred active nests. Gardiners Island has been under the ownership of the Gardiner family since 1639, when the first Gardiner purchased this eight-mile-long island from the Montauk Indians for a few Dutch blankets, powder and shot, rum, and a gun. It has been privately owned ever since, and so it is almost completely wild. Thus ospreys have had optimal opportunities to breed there.

My first visit to the island in 1948 was an exciting experience; I saw so many ospreys nesting contentendly, as well as a large heronry, plus dozens of geese, turkeys, and other spectacular wild birds breeding under ideal conditions. This was a great treat. I managed to obtain permission from the family to visit the island at least once every year and so began to take a deep interest in the osprey population there.

During the war, troops in the South Pacific and other tropical areas were confronted with the great problem of endeavoring to remain healthy in areas where malaria was highly prevalent. Great efforts were made by the military to control the mosquitoes carrying this disease. A chemical synthesized in a German laboratory, many years before, had for a long time been a chemical curiosity but was subsequently found to be highly lethal to many species of insect. And so DDT, its full technical name dichlorodiphenyltrichloroethane, was put into high production and used extensively throughout many of the South Pacific islands, New Guinea, and the Philippines. It was very effective; it killed mosquitoes. So at the end of World War II it was hailed as the great panacea for all our problems with insect pests. DDT went into higher production than ever before, and very soon planes were seen in all agricultural areas, generously spraying the terrain with this chemical. For a while this World War II hero was welcomed by almost everyone. DDT is one of the pesticides in the family of chlorinated hydrocarbons, which includes endrin, aldrin, toxaphene, heptachlor, lindane, chlordane, and mirex.

It took the immense courage and ability of one small woman to begin the campaign against these insidious, widespread poisons. Rachel Carson, a marine biologist who had already written several beautifully eloquent books on the subject of marine life, was enlisted by a group of environmentalists to warn the world what was happening to many organisms that were not the intended targets of this broad-spectrum, long-living chemical that was invading the worldwide environment. Her book *Silent Spring*, published in 1961, is surely one of the great books of the twentieth century, in that it was the first indictment of persistent chemicals that have done so much to harm nontarget organisms of many kinds and, in all probability, the human race itself.

This book aroused the ire of the chemical industry, and Rachel Carson was viciously attacked as a hysterical woman who didn't know what she was talking about. Even her private life was attacked. But through it all she maintained a courageous silence, and since then all she had stated so eloquently has been proved, although at that time not even she was aware of all the effects that DDT and other similar chemicals were having on nontarget organisms.

In my studies of osprey populations on Gardiners Island it was obvious by the early fifties that something was going wrong. They were not producing as many young as in former years. By the end of the decade, osprey populations were collapsing everywhere. When Rachel Carson's book came out, I realized that ospreys were being affected by DDT, and this was why their reproductive success was dropping drastically and why the breeding population itself was also dwindling. From the estimated three hundred nests on Gardiners Island during the late forties there were only about fifty-five active nests on the island by the mid-sixties. The entire colony was producing a total of 2 or 3 young at the most instead of the average of 2.2 per active nest, which had been the norm up until the advent of DDT. It was also noticeable that many eggs were dented and cracked by the weight of the incubating bird. Studies on the peregrine falcon in Britain indicated that DDT was interfering with the metabolism of sufficient calcium carbonate to produce a healthy eggshell, and comparisons with pre-DDT eggs in old collections showed that this was indeed the case. This appeared also to be the case with the osprey.

I began taking overdue eggs back to the laboratory and having them analyzed by gas chromatography, and sure enough, gross amounts of DDT, as much as twenty parts per million wet weight, were found in these eggs, enough to prevent the development of a healthy embryo. There were indications that DDT was affecting other non-target organisms. In the Great South Bay, Brookhaven scientists were finding massive amounts of DDT in fish, crab larvae, and even marine plant life. It is worth considering why DDT is such a pervasive, broad-spectrum poison. In the first place, it has the characteristic of mobility. When DDT is sprayed from the air the sprayer is fortunate if as much as 30 percent of it reaches the target. The rest of it is picked up in the atmosphere and can be transported for hundreds or thousands of miles. That is why DDT is found in the tissues of Adélie penguins and crabeater seals in the Antarctic, thousands of miles from the nearest source of application. Second, this molecule does not break down quickly, and since it is a new material to be introduced into living organisms, they are unable to metabolize it readily. Two of the products that result eventually, DDD and DDE, retain many of the biological characteristics of the parent. Curiously enough, while DDE has little effect on insects, it is highly toxic to birds and is perceived to be more persistent than DDT. That is why it is so widely spread in the environment. The third characteristic of DDT is its solubility, which is extremely low in water, but very high in the lipid or fatty tissues that exist in all living organisms. Thus a molecule suspended in an aqueous system is taken up by the first creature coming in contact with it and is thereby transferred from an inorganic environment to an organic one. Combining these first three properties: mobility, stability, and solubility in fatty tissues, we find that DDT is

173

able to move through food chains from one organism to another at each link, thus becoming more highly concentrated.

In a typical but simplified example of this process, known as biological magnification, we find that planktonic animals in the lake have gathered DDT into their systems at levels of a few hundredths of a part per million (PPM). These creatures are consumed by minnows with levels of a quarter of a PPM; the minnows, in turn, are eaten by needlefish, which are carrying several PPM. Larger carnivorous fish have now concentrated the DDT residues at hundreds of PPMs and carnivorous birds, such as ospreys and eagles, carry even higher concentrations. Thus these top carnivores have accumulated DDT residues as much as a million times as great as the concentrations in the lake that was originally sprayed. This is the reason many of the raptorial and insectivorous birds and carnivorous fish were suffering catastrophic declines in population.

After *Silent Spring* was published, it was learned that chlorinated hydrocarbons, in addition to acting as nerve toxins, also induced enzymes that break down estrogen, a female steroid sex hormone. Since estrogen is known to play an important role in mediating calcium metabolism, the pesticide interferes with the production of calcium for the formation of eggshell. Therefore, birds carrying high concentrations of DDT were laying thin-shelled eggs that broke down under the weight of the incubating bird or lost so much water that the embryo died before hatching. Such birds as bald eagles and brown pelicans, in many cases unable to metabolize any calcium, were producing eggs with no shell at all. In 1970, only a single pelican chick was fledged at the large colony on Anacapa Island off the California coast. This was because of an effluent rich in DDT from the Montrose Chemical Company plant, which was the main manufacturer of the pesticide at that time. It was found that the Montrose waste water was being dumped into the Los Angeles sewer system. As if a further indictment were needed, a number of laboratory experiments showed that DDT induced cancer in rats, mice, and trout. This indicates a high probability that it can be carcinogenic in humans.

At that time we had a small organization concerned with local environmental issues known as the Brookhaven Town Natural Resources Committee. When confronted with the problems caused by DDT and other members of this family of chemicals, we determined to try to prevent further use of them in our local environment. The main user of DDT on Long Island, at that time, was the Suffolk County Mosquito Control Commission (SCMCC). We appealed to them, but they ignored our arguments; they reasoned that DDT was cheap, it killed mosquitoes, and it was easy to apply. Its effect on other organisms was not their concern. We then appealed to New York State authorities in Albany, and again, no helpful response. It seemed that the courtroom was the only way in which we could hope to attain any success. A local lawyer, Victor Yannacone, was eager to try his mettle in a class-action mandamus. In this type of lawsuit no damages are demanded, but the petition asks for a court order, in our case to force the SCMCC to cease and desist from spraying DDT.

The papers were prepared, and we found no shortage of strong scientific evidence that DDT was indeed a powerful contaminant affecting many nontarget organisms.

Victor Yannacone decided that in order to make an ecologist out of the judge hearing the case we would need a set of food-web charts showing how DDT was transmitted throughout an entire ecosystem. I worked one whole weekend to produce a set of seven food-web charts depicting the principal organisms in seven of the most important Suffolk County ecosystems, such as salt bays, salt marshes, deciduous woods, developed areas, pine-oaks scrub, old fields, and freshwater ponds.

The case was heard in the New York State Supreme Court in Riverhead in November 1966. In six days of testimony we were able to convince the court that our case was a good one. In fact, the judge himself, an old bayman, remarked on the fact that the blueclaw crab, a valuable resource in the Great South Bay, had almost disappeared within recent years and that DDT was the likely culprit, since our testimony showed that DDT in a few parts per billion in bay water was lethal to crab larvae. In the cross-examination, we were able to show that DDT was losing some of its effectiveness, because insects like mosquitoes, with their rapid life cycles, can produce resistant strains in a very few years. Thus the head of the SCMCC was forced in cross-examination to admit that in some areas as much as eight times as much DDT was needed to obtain the same results as had been the case originally. The counsel for the defense was hard put to summon any valid scientific support for the necessity of using DDT for mosquito control or to show that it was harmless to nontarget organisms. In fact, any ecological arguments in favor of DDT were nonexistent. Thus the court imposed an injunction on DDT use by the defendant, and we were victorious. DDT has not been used by the SCMCC since that court action in 1966.

We then realized that the courtroom was to be the scene of many future battles in defending the environment. In view of the unusual character of the case, it received nationwide attention, and soon we were being bombarded with requests for help from many different quarters. We had to turn down most of these requests; we all had our regular jobs at Brookhaven National Laboratory and the State University of New York at Stony Brook, and the only way we could help was to use up vacation time. As a forerunner to the official beginning of the nationwide environmental movement in 1970, we held a critical meeting at Brookhaven Laboratory in late 1967 and decided to incorporate, and thus the Environmental Defense Fund (EDF) was founded. It grew rapidly, although in the early days we were extremely short of funds and whimsically referred to ourselves as the Fundless Environmental Defenders. Because of my gray hair, which might give an aura of respectability to what many considered a radical group, I was elected chairman of the board of trustees, a position I held for the next five years.

Funds, staff, office space, and equipment had to be found for survival. The random donations we were receiving to date were just sufficient to support current litigation but gave no promise for continuity. The National Audubon Society, however, had from the start taken great interest in the EDF approach and was able, through its Rachel Carson Memorial Fund, to give us some sense of permanence by providing funds for legal counsel's salary and some office facilities and some part-time secretarial help.

Our first office was the one-room attic over the Stony Brook post office. Stony Brook is a charming little town; the business area, fronted by an immaculate village green, has been remodeled in the Colonial style. All the shops and offices have window boxes, and there are flower beds and shade trees everywhere. But it is the post office that is the central feature of the town. The EDF office was located directly behind a life-size replica of a bald eagle that flaps its outstretched wings to count the hours. At noon every day a crowd gathers below to watch that eagle give twelve majestic flaps, while from the nearby firehouse the siren gives an earsplitting shriek, much to the consternation of anyone who happens to be involved in a telephone conversation with the people in the EDF office.

Once granted tax-exempt status by the Internal Revenue Service, EDF launched a drive for funds and approached several foundations in the hope of receiving long-term grants. Our reception here was not too encouraging at first. EDF's guerrilla style, lack of conventional organization, and head-on approach were not "respectable." But though EDF was hampered by lack of funds, it did not lack for potential cases. Appeals for aid in fighting environmental threats of many kinds were pouring in, most of these were worthy causes, and it was difficult and even painful to refuse to take them.

With the coming of Rod Cameron as EDF's executive director in 1969, a proposal for a substantial grant from the Ford Foundation was prepared. But to convince foundations that a grant to us would be a helping hand to get started, rather than a permanent dole or a flash in the pan, it was necessary for us to implement a public membership drive. At that juncture, in the early spring of 1970, we had only enough funds to meet our meager payroll for several months. We did, however, have a powerful message for everyone in the nation, and we decided to gamble everything on a three-quarter-page advertisement in the Sunday *New York Times*.

It had been found during EDF's battles with DDT that mother's milk in the United States was averaging seven times as much DDT as was permitted in marketable cow's milk. We had a wry joke to the effect that if mother's milk was in any other container, it would be illegal to transport it across state lines. As luck would have it, with perhaps the gods of the environment playing their part, this dramatic message, along with a photograph of a mother with an infant at her breast and an invitation to become a member of EDF, appeared on as nasty a March day as could be imagined. Snow mixed with freezing rain fell all morning, with the result that people stayed inside and went through the *Times* from beginning to end. The results were heartening; not only did we recover the cost of the advertisement with several thousands to spare, but we were entering a new and more stable growth phase for EDF. With Rod Cameron's fine leadership and the full support of the executive committee, we could begin hiring more professional staff—scientists and lawyers. A grant from the Ford Foundation for $285,000 was now forthcoming, and we were on our way.

By June 1970, we had sufficient finances to make a much-needed move from the tiny attic of the Stony Brook post office. A fine 100-year-old farmhouse was located in nearby East Setauket; it was somewhat run-down and the front porch sagged precariously, but it had a grand old-fashioned stove and plenty of rooms to accommodate our growing staff. There was also a sizable yard, so a plot could be cultivated for staff so they could raise their own vegetables in the summer. We remained there until 1977, by which time we had opened offices in Washington, D.C., and California, and it was becoming increasingly important to move the head office into New York City.

Unfortunately, DDT is still in use in many other nations, although its effectiveness has decreased enormously. Insects, with their rapid life cycles, can build up resistant strains in a matter of a few years, as became evident during cross-examination in our original DDT trial.

The whole point of the use of a broad-spectrum, persistent chemical like DDT as well as many of the other chlorinated hydrocarbons, which have the same general characteristics, is like using a torpedo to attack the liner *Queen Elizabeth* to get rid of the rats on board.

In 1970, a statewide ban on DDT and many other of the persistent broad-spectrum pesticides was imposed by New York State's governor. And eventually, in 1972, in lengthy hearings involving testimony by EDF scientists, there was a nationwide ban on the further use of the chemical.

Since then, levels in the tissues of ospreys, bald eagles, and other creatures at the top of the food chains, as well as in man himself, have been declining slowly. During our battle against this pesticide, Joseph Hickey, a noted naturalist, predicted that within the next ten years the osprey would be gone in the northeastern United States. I would certainly have agreed with him at that time, but following the decrease in the use of this chemical, levels have gone down drastically, and recent checks on osprey productivity on such areas as Gardiners Island have revealed that now they are having a reproductive success of almost two chicks per active nest. It has been a long, drawn-out battle, but it has been a striking example of what can be done by a combination of good science and good law when a symbol such as the osprey is drastically affected. And now we have a pair of ospreys nesting at the edge of our marsh, so we can watch them busy with their domestic duties right from our backyard.

Since the DDT case, EDF has come a long way. With a budget of over $25 million a year we are now involved in many environmental issues, such as water resources, land use, wildlife, acid rain, man-made carcinogens, and wetlands. Not only is EDF involved in national problems; it is becoming engaged in the battle to prevent further destruction of the ozone layer, which has been so significant a phenomenon in Antarctica and now in the Arctic.

Global warming, the so-called greenhouse effect, is also of concern to EDF scientists. We are also involved in habitat protection in other parts of the world and are pressuring the World Bank and other international financial organizations to reduce the emphasis on large-scale forest destruction and dam-building projects that are so environmentally destructive. Although I am still a trustee emeritus, I am no longer as active as I was. I served as chairman for five years and then turned the running of the organization over to other far more competent people than myself, but it has been a great pleasure and a privilege to see the growth of this organization and to know of the many victories it has achieved in the struggle for a better world to hand over to future generations.

11

Heading Back to Sea

At the end of 1970 I reached the mandatory retirement age of sixty-five, since my birthday came on December 30. I was now free to devote more time to the EDF and many other projects and interests as well as to my own family, although, of course, the children were now all grown up. My strongest interests were awaiting me. One way in which to increase my activities in the fields of travel and wildlife study was to serve as a naturalist on some of the ornithologically oriented tours that were developing. One of our early EDF trustees was Roland Clement, who until his retirement was chief biologist for the National Audubon Society. He became a good friend and was able to find for me an assignment leading some of the National Audubon ecology tours to such attractive parts of the world as southeast Alaska, the Galápagos, Patagonia, and the Caribbean. I did these trips for several years. They usually involved groups of about thirty people. Then I received word that sixteen berths had been reserved for National Audubon members on a vessel called the *Lindblad Explorer* to go to Antarctica.

I had never been to that part of the world, but when asked to lead this group, I eagerly accepted. I had several months in which I could study up on the wildlife we could expect to encounter there. I found that Robert Cushman Murphy's two-volume monograph, *Oceanic Birds of South America*, was an extremely useful source of information for me. And so, by the time the expedition came to pass, I was able to speak fairly knowledgeably about birds and other animals I had never encountered before. The group was an extremely eager one, and before we even reached the town of Ushuaia in Tierra del Fuego, we were all good friends. After a long bus trip from the airport across the mountains, we were able to board our ship at this southern port on the Beagle Channel, and I at once fell under the spell of this sturdy little vessel. I was also delighted to find that I was sharing a cabin with none other than Keith Shackleton, a man I had never met but for whom I had already developed a tremendous admiration. He is a talented artist, a fine naturalist, and a superb shipmate, and we very quickly became fast friends. He was already passionately in love with the areas to which we were heading, and I could not have had a better cabinmate with whom to see this new part of the world. We went first to the Falklands, 600 miles east of Tierra del Fuego, themselves rich in wildlife of many kinds.

These islands have been compared to the Shetlands, off the northern tip of Scotland. The terrain consists mainly of rolling grass and heath-covered hills, known as "hard camp," and low-lying boggy areas known as "soft camp." They are treeless, except for a few introduced species, mainly the Monterey cypress. The air is generally clear, crisp, and exhilarating, and one feels like walking endlessly over the springy turf. There are two large islands in the group, East and West Falkland, and about two hundred smaller ones, a few of which have human settlements.

Sheep farming is the main industry; the constant strong, cool winds produce wool of exceptionally fine quality. The islanders, known as Kelpers, are splendid, friendly people, but they are very much set in their ways.

It has been said that they eat mutton 364 days of the year and on Christmas Day they eat lamb. Their main source of fuel is peat, which is cut out of the upland heaths. There is only one settlement worthy of calling itself a town; that is Port Stanley, on East Falkland, the seat of government, with a population of 800 and several fine British-type pubs. The rest of the population, of about one thousand, is thinly scattered over the rest of the archipelago.

Although land birds occur at a rather low density, the Falklands are abundantly rich in seabirds, waterfowl, and shorebirds. Teeming colonies of rockhopper, gentoo, and Magellanic penguins occur on many of the islands, and there is an ever-growing colony of about two hundred king penguins on East Falkland, after this handsome bird was almost exterminated from the archipelago by 1870. Black-browed albatroses breed on several islands in very large colonies. These magnificent birds build pedestal-shaped nests of mud where they rear their single chicks, and allow a close human approach without losing any of their aloof dignity. Then there are several species of waterfowl, including the handsome upland, ruddy-headed, and ashy-headed geese. One of the most interesting species of duck is the flightless steamer duck, named after the old side-wheel paddle steamers. This heavy-bodied bird, unable to rise from the water, flails the surface with its stubby wings, making a great commotion. Several species of shearwater, prion, cormorant, storm petrel, and diving petrel also breed on these islands.

Marine mammal life is represented by elephant seals, fur seals, and sea lions. Several species of small dolphins occur in the surrounding waters, including the friendly, playful little black and white Commerson's dolphin, locally known as puffing pig.

While I fell in love with the Falklands and its wildlife, it was Antarctica itself that had the greatest impact on me. We were seeing this part of the world under ideal conditions. The ship itself, 250 feet long, with an ice-strengthened bow, a double hull, a single propeller well protected from ice, and a maximum passenger capacity of about ninety, was ideal for visiting Antarctica. In a few days one came to know everyone on board, and it was almost like cruising on a large yacht.

I feel it is true that no one can visit Antarctica without being deeply affected by it, in many ways that are hard to explain. It is perhaps the combination of the grandeur, the majesty, its unspoiled, almost innocent aspect, along with the fact that man has not yet succeeded in taming it and it is still largely unaffected by man's impact, although, subsequently, one wonders how long it will be able to survive now that so many nations are eyeing it with eagerness, sparked by the desire to exploit its natural resources. Nonetheless, it is a very exciting part of the world, and after this first visit I was consumed with the desire to learn more about it by making subsequent visits.

The penguins themselves are fascinating creatures to study. Perhaps one is at first primarily affected by their somewhat comical appearance on land. They have a quizzical air that indicates a kind of fearless curiosity, but when one considers the extremely harsh environment in which they are obliged to live one becomes filled with admiration for them. That they can not only survive but live successfully in their enormous colonies is a tribute to their astonishing adaptability.

Perhaps the most impressive of the seventeen species existing in the world is the king penguin. The first sight of one of these creatures is almost breathtaking. Not only was it larger than any of the other penguins we had encountered; it was also far more colorful in a part of the world where the normal colors for most birds are combinations of black, brown, gray, and white. This bird, with its resplendent orange ear patch, brilliant orange breast fading into a glorious lemon yellow, and its regal steel blue back, is strikingly beautiful, and the bird itself has an air of dignity that adds to its majesty. One has only to sit down in front of a few of these birds and they will approach in a very nonaggressive manner, regarding one curiously, perhaps examining one's feet, but at all times maintaining an air of somewhat aloof politeness.

That first cruise was a great success. And very soon afterward the Lindblad Travel Company, which at that time was responsible for operating the ship, contacted me to offer me a post as naturalist and lecturer on board. I was delighted to accept this offer. The Audubon tours had been very pleasant, but on these trips one is not only tour leader; one is also baggage master, ticket holder, confidant, shepherd, and recipient of all problems and complaints. It means frequently shuttling from hotel, to bus, to plane, to motel, to cruise vessel, and back to overnight accommodations, so one is always on the move, involving packing, repacking, handling of baggage, having to account for all pieces of baggage, plus having to be sure that every passenger has awakened in time, so one must worry constantly about problems other than identifying birds, mammals, and plants.

To serve as naturalist on a ship like the *Lindblad Explorer* was a great delight, for one is thus relieved from all responsibilities regarding passengers and their possessions once one is on board. They can come or go as they please on the landings, and once their baggage is on board, one has no more concern about that. There was no question about my accepting this wonderful offer.

Soon I was traveling on this grand little ship to Alaska, the South Pacific, Indonesia, New Zealand, Australia, and many other parts of the world. By using large Zodiacs we did not need to tie up at docks except at the beginning and end of the cruises, most of which lasted for about two weeks, but some for as much as four weeks. With the Zodiacs, we could land on coral reefs or on beaches through a reasonable surf without any problems. These rubber-bodied, air-inflated craft are extremely seaworthy, and having flexible sides and bottoms they can absorb the sharp points of rock and coral without suffering the type of damage that would occur on a rigid-hulled landing craft. Thus we can visit areas that are not accessible to the large cruise ships.

In any case, the type of people that come on such cruises are far from the usual tourist, who wishes to see art galleries and cathedrals and shop for postcards, T-shirts, and souvenirs. We are able to visit the more unspoiled parts of the world, where the main emphasis is on scenery, primitive cultures, wildlife, and botany.

There are usually a group of half a dozen people on the staff, specialists in one field or another, who lecture on subjects relating to the places we are visiting, so our passengers receive an education in a variety of fields. We are also able to establish friendships with people in more remote parts of the world, especially when we return to an area that we have visited before. I feel that I have become far more of a citizen of the world than formerly.

In 1984, I participated in a truly historic cruise, the first voyage of a cruise vessel through the Northwest Passage, starting from Newfoundland and ending in Yokohama forty-two days later. This was somewhat of a gamble, since there is a great deal of ice to contend with and sometimes the channels through which we would have to pass would be completely blocked. We did, however, have an experienced icemaster, Canadian captain Tom Pullen, on board. The icemaster has an important function in making a successful passage in an area like the Northwest Passage, where pack ice is always on the move at the behest of wind and current and where a passage free at one time can be blocked quickly a few hours later.

It is critical to make the most difficult part of the transit at the time of maximum ice breakup and before new ice is forming, and this is in the early part of September. We had a maximum number of passengers on board on this cruise, and there was even a long wait list with many disappointed applicants for whom there was no room. We had actually a total of ninety-eight on board who were willing to take the gamble. Of the many voyages I've made on this fine little vessel this one was unquestionably the most exciting.

We started from Saint John's in Newfoundland, with a very fine send-off from the local citizenry, together with a troop dressed in the scarlet uniforms of the old Newfoundland regiment, who even fired some ancient cannons in our honor. Sailing from Saint John's on August 20, we followed the west coast of Greenland northward from Narssuaq to Jakobshaven, and from Disko Island we crossed Baffin Bay to visit some of the spectacular fiords of northern Baffin Island. We then passed through the small Inuit settlement of Pond Inlet and around Bylot

Island to Lancaster Sound, which was the real start of the Northwest Passage. We went from there westward to Beechey Island, off the southwest coast of Devon Island. Here the ill-fated expedition led by Sir John Franklin in 1845 in his two ships *Erebus* and *Terror* wintered before proceeding onward. We landed upon this desolate spot and found three graves of members of the expedition. One grave, opened by Canadian archaeologists, revealed the body of a young sailor perfectly preserved by the permafrost.

Franklin's two ships subsequently reached King William Island, but here they were beset and crushed by the ice. None of the 128 men ever survived to reach civilization. Numerous later expeditions searched for the missing men and their ships and thus much of the Northwest Passage was found to exist, but it was still impassable for contemporary ships.

It was Roald Amundsen in 1904 who set out in his ship *Gjoa* to complete the first transit of the passage, but it took him three years to do it, as he was obliged to overwinter in the ice for two seasons before he finally got through to the Beaufort Sea and reached Alaska. Other vessels have made the transit since. One was the big tanker *Manhattan*, but she was escorted by a fleet of ice-breakers, and it was Tom Pullen who was icemaster on that historic passage.

From Resolute we turned southward through Peel Sound and made a side trip through Bellot Strait to Fort Ross and Point Zenith near Fort Ross. Here we reached the northernmost tip of the entire North American continent. Since I had already landed on Cape Horn, I could now claim that I had truly seen the ends of the Earth. At Fort Ross we had an exciting experience with a polar bear. We had landed the passengers to visit an abandoned Hudson Bay Company station, but some of us went off ahead and over the brow of the hill we saw an adult polar bear quite close by. We had to dash back and round up all the passengers to get to the Zodiacs as fast as possible.

In James Ross Strait we sent a Zodiac on ahead with sounding equipment and were able to find a deeper channel hitherto unknown and charted the passage for use by future shipping. We stopped at several small Inuit settlements, and then, going south of King William Island, a better route than the one taken by Franklin, since he had been trapped on the north side of the island by heavy ice, we went westward again through Simpson Strait and Coronation Gulf, passing on the south side of Victoria Island.

Once we reached the Beaufort Sea we encountered heavy pack ice, which completely covered the sea ahead of us, and eventually we had to retreat sixty miles. Our captain, however, took a gamble and found a passage inside the ice, very close to the shoreline, with only a foot of water under the keel at times. We eventually got through, and when we reached Point Barrow, in Alaska, we realized that our problems with ice were over.

There were forty-eight cases of champagne on board, and since the ship was to be sold to another company once we reached Japan, we were determined that at least none of that champagne would be part of the transfer. So from then on it was a continuous champagne party celebrating the historic passage. We were actually three days ahead of the planned itinerary by the time we reached Point Barrow, so we had more time to spend in the Aleutian Islands and thus reached Yokohama forty-two days after we had set out from Newfoundland. In addition to the euphoria at having accomplished this historic passage, our arrival was tinged with sadness, because we knew, with the ship being sold to another company, the staff itself would scatter. To this was added the sadness of seeing the ship we had come to love on so many voyages passing out of the hands of the company for which we had been working.

It was a poignant moment when we left the ship at Yokohama and headed our separate ways homeward. We felt this was the end of an era, but it was far from being the end of my career at sea. For since then I have served as naturalist and lecturer not only on the *Explorer*, but on a number of other vessels as well. These voyages have enriched my life in so many extraordinary ways. Not only have I been exposed to more superb scenery and more rich concentrations of wildlife than anyone could reasonably hope for; I have also been able to establish great and lasting friendships. It has also been my privilege to have had some of my children and grandchildren along on these voyages. My daughter Jennifer has been on several. In fact, this is where she met her husband, Peter Clement, since he was quartermaster on board during an Antarctic cruise on which she accompanied me some years ago. Also, my second son, Peter, has been my shipmate on many cruises, serving as an expert boatman and a superb naturalist. It has been a special pleasure having him as shipmate and cabinmate.

I have made lasting friendships with more people on the lecture staff than I can venture to name, such fine men as Keith Shackleton, Alan Gurney, Peter Butz, Jim Snyder, Peter Harrison, Tom Ritchie, Mike McDowell, and many other who share with me the thrill of visiting these exciting parts of the world.

One of my functions on these cruises is to maintain a log describing the day's events for the passengers. I illustrate this with sketches of the wildlife and plants that we see in addition to scenery and other features of interest. The original goes back to the office responsible for the cruise, and in several weeks copies are made, including color reproductions of all the sketches, and these are sent to all the participating passengers, ship's officers, and staff. This has been a very rewarding assignment for me, and I have received many letters of thanks from past shipmates for these records.

During the past eighteen years, I have served as naturalist and lecturer on a variety of small vessels that accommodated anywhere from 40 to 160 passengers. Unquestionably the most impressive was the *Sea Cloud*, a magnificent four-masted square-rigged bark of 2,440 tons, with an overall length of 254 feet. She was once owned by the late Marjorie Merriweather Post, the cereal heiress. The ship has had a long and varied career and is currently owned by a German company that has her available for charter. With a total of thirty sails, she is a splendid sight under full canvas. I maintain that a square-rigged sailing vessel is one of man's most beautiful and efficient creations, and it is sad that we cannot see these superb vessels more often.

The ship I have cruised on far more than any other is the motor ship *Linblad Explorer*, recently renamed *Society Explorer*. She is 250 feet long; with her reinforced bow and single propeller she is ideally suited for operation in Arctic and Antarctic waters, where it is often necessary to pass through fields of heavy pack ice. She is just the right size and has all the excellent seagoing qualities that enable her to cruise capably in the often storm-lashed seas of the higher latitudes. I have made thirty-five cruises to Antarctica, a part of the world that I have come to love with a deep passion. But between the Antarctic summers, November to March, and the Arctic summers, June to September, the cruises are generally taken in more tropical waters, though the circumnavigation of the British Isles and the cruises up the coast of Norway are always popular with passengers. Other outstanding parts of the world are southeast Alaska, Baja California, and the Orinoco and Amazon Rivers. I have made many visits to these areas and have come to know them well. The more one visits an area, the more familiar one becomes with its flora and fauna, its people, and its character. So I never tire of returning to these places; all have their own charm and interest, and once I know what to look for they have an increased meaning to me.

12

Shipmates

In addition to the many enjoyable and exciting experiences, a further pleasure is derived from the friendships made with the people who join these voyages. Passengers come in all shapes, sizes, backgrounds, and ages, and it is an endless source of interest to study them and learn more about them. Most of them, naturally, are elderly, since these are mainly the ones who can afford both the time and the money to come on these cruises, which run anywhere from ten to forty days in length. There is never a cruise when one does not find at least one truly fascinating individual. There are a few that might be considered objectionable, but very few indeed. We do have some complainers and these can be very upsetting, but they are few and far between.

Most of our shipmates are enthusiastic, interested, and far from the run-of-the-mill tourist. They are more interested in seeing the wild places of the world. Or perhaps they have become satiated with that other type of travel that is provided on the larger cruise ships, with their entertainment officers, their shuffleboard, their 11:00 A.M. bouillon, and their deck chairs arrayed in long monotonous rows. Our passengers are interested in learning more about the wild creatures with which we share the Earth. Many times I've had one say that if he or she can just see a polar bear in the wild he or she will be satisfied, or perhaps it is a walrus or a whale or a wild monkey or a toucan.

In tropical waters, we teach them how to snorkle and even to scuba dive, and there they are introduced to an entirely new world. This is a world of brilliantly colored reef fish of many species, as well as sea turtles, dugongs, and yes, even sharks. For these tropical island cruises, we always have on our staff people who are well experienced in underwater biology and photography. Sometimes we have had the privilege of the company of the late Sir Peter Scott, certainly an outstanding naturalist in many fields, but particularly in marine biology. I have seen Peter sit on the bottom, among the corals, and with his water pencil and pad write down the scientific names of well over a hundred species of fish observed within a period of an hour.

I have seen Ron and Valerie Taylor, the two great Australian marine biologists and photographers, feeding quite large sharks, and I've had my own granddaughters participating in these activities. Carin, Shelly, and Lyda have all learned how to scuba dive under the tutelage of Valerie, who deserves mention as one of the most remarkable women I've ever met. She is utterly fearless in the water, but at the same time, she is still blue-eyed, blond, shapely, and almost fragile-looking. Valerie does not look at all like someone who invites attacks by great white sharks when testing out the coat-of-mail type vest she designed, but she is that kind of person. And Ron, shy and reserved in contrast to the ebullient Valerie, is an outstanding man in underwater photography. He designs and makes all his own equipment and has the respect of every tropical scuba diver.

And Keith Shackleton, distant relative of the great Antarctic explorer, has been my shipmate on many cruises, particularly those to Antarctica. A brilliant artist, a fine naturalist, and, best of all, superb human being,

Keith is modest about his lecturing ability, but to me he is one of the best, in his whimsical way. Give Keith a blackboard and a piece of chalk, and he will bring it to life with a few deft sweeps of his hand: a gull, a whale, a seal will appear like magic on the board. He makes my own feeble efforts in that direction appear pitiful. Yet he is extraordinarily diffident about his talents, which is perhaps one of his most appealing characteristics. He is without a doubt one of the most popular persons on board, and it is my great regret that in recent years our paths have separated. Keith has been obliged to spend more time at the easel and less on the ship. But with his talents he should be given maximum time with his paints.

But it is the passengers that are in many ways even more fascinating. We come to know them well when they return again and again, and this is one of the great pleasures of these cruises, to get to know these people as warm friends with whom we have shared many experiences. I can remember one lively little woman who came regularly on these voyages some years ago. Although she was well into her eighties, she was always full of energy, taking delight in all the creatures she saw, with a wide-eyed air of schoolgirl wonder. Someone once likened her to a chipmunk; she had that kind of quick and alert air about her. For the sake of anonymity, let us call her Mary Brown. She would often be seen trotting around the decks while we were at sea, and she would always be ready for the first boat when we were preparing for a landing. I was curious about her background, and upon checking the passenger information file, I was astonished to find that she gave as her address an almshouse in Kent, England.

So when I came to know her better, I asked her how she managed to travel on these quite expensive cruises and yet lives in a home for the indigent. With a coy giggle, she confided in me that she had some funds tucked away in a Canadian bank that the British government was unaware of. "But, Mary," I said, "what do you tell the folks in the almshouse when you are about to leave on one of these cruises?" "Oh," she replied with a twinkle in her eyes, "I tell them I have to take care of a sick cousin on the Isle of Wight." And so, with the mythical cousin suffering from another setback every few months, Mary would be back on board and as chipper as ever. She was firmly convinced that all wild birds have a craving for bread, so at mealtime she would stuff some extra rolls in her capacious reticule. These would then be offered to penguins, albatrosses, petrels, elephant seals, or any other creature she encountered on shore. She never seemed to notice that her gifts were ignored, since these creatures did not even recognize bread as food. On Enderby Island, in the Auckland Islands, south of New Zealand, some well-meaning British officers had, long ago, released rabbits to serve as emergency food for castaways. The animals have prospered, and their burrows are everywhere. While strolling ashore with a group, I happened to glance into a rabbit burrow entrance and was surprised to see a carrot lying there. A further check revealed the same condition in every burrow. Then the light dawned; Mary had been at work.

On Carcass Island in the Falklands, Keith Shackleton and I knew of a peregrine falcon nest at the top of a mountain. Wishing to check on it, we were headed up the slope when we noticed Mary behind us struggling gamely to keep up, so we waited and told her of our mission. "May I come, too?" she asked. So up we went. Reaching the summit, we encountered a howling wind, a common condition in the Falklands. We were concerned that Mary would be blown away, she looked so small and fragile. So when we reached a sheep fence, Keith gallantly picked her up and passed her over. That night in the lounge I happened to hear her recounting the adventure to several ladies. "And then," she said in ecstatic tones, "Keith Shackleton held me in his arms."

On one cruise we made up certificates for all those who had crossed the Antarctic Circle for the first time. I could not resist a little joke, so Mary's certificate certified that she had circumnavigated the Isle of Wight and that the southernmost latitude she had attained was fifty degrees, thirty minutes north. Mary went along with this gentle leg-pull, her eyes sparkling with delight. Sadly, we have not seen Mary for the past few years. Have the authorities caught up with her at last, or has she settled down with her exciting memories in the almshouse? I miss this wonderful little lady who, on her own, outwitted the might of Her Majesty's government for so many years.

Japanese tourists seem to go everywhere these days, and we have had a fair quota of them on the ship. Some of them have become quite Westernized. But a few still possess, for us at least, the inscrutability of the Orient in ways that are baffling. I recall a perfect day at Cape Adare, in the Ross Sea, Antarctica. We had found a landing site on a snowbank at the foot of a glacier. It was one of those perfectly still days, so the scenery was at its majestic best. We decided to hold a champagne party. A Zodiac brought the champagne and the necessary glasses from the ship, and we stood around enjoying this in the companionship of our shipmates. Among us was a small elderly Japanese gentleman who kept very much to himself and rarely spoke. We happened to notice him walking off a short distance, and we were curious enough to wonder what he planned to do. When he was less than one hundred feet away, he turned his back to us, unzipped his pants, and proceeded to urinate in the snow, forming some Japanese characters. But this was not the end of it, for when he had zipped up his pants, he brought out his camera and photographed the artistic creation. After this, he returned quietly to our group as if nothing had happened. It was a long time before we recovered from this extraordinary scene.

Then there was the Egg Slurper. We gave him this name because of his unique technique in consuming fried eggs. He was another very solitary Japenese who breakfasted alone. And we never took much notice of him until Keith nudged me one morning, advising me to watch the man closely when he was brought two fried eggs. For a few moments he gazed fixedly at the plate; then slowly his face moved closer to the objective. Suddenly he struck with the swiftness and accuracy of a cobra. There was a distinct sucking sound, and as his head came up, we could see that one of the eggs was gone. A few moments later the other egg also disappeared just as abruptly. From then on our own breakfasts were forgotten temporarily as we secretly watched this extraordinary routine.

There was a tiny Japanese lady we called the Giant Microbe. She was determined to be in the first Zodiac whenever a landing was to be made, and regardless of how full the lobby might be, with everyone waiting to take their turn, the Giant Microbe would wriggle her way between the legs of the giants all around her and would eventually end up in the forefront of the landing party. It was inevitable that she succeeded in this. What inclined her to be so determined to be first we could never figure.

Sometimes we have had very overweight people who have their own problems. At times one must be a bit of an athlete to get in and out of the Zodiac when there is a heavy swell running, as the Zodiac rides up and down at the loading platform. And while there are plenty of experienced sailors to help, handling a very heavy person is not always easy. I remember one who was invariably paralyzed when she got to the gangway, ready to make that final step into the boat. She was a very large-bodied woman with a tiny head mounted on this huge mass of flesh, and on the very top of her head was a baseball cap. Sometimes it took as many as five strong seamen to get her in and out of the Zodiac. I often wondered why she chose a small vessel such as ours, with its often-bobbing Zodiacs, when she could have chosen one of the big cruise ships, where she could have walked comfortably down a gangway onto a nice, steady dock to make a landing. She insisted on coming along, and on one occasion I remember her being caught in a big roll of the ship and hurled bodily from one side of the dining room to the other, ending up crashing into one of the circular tables. It has been bent on its pedestal ever since. People like this can never be forgotten.

There was another very heavy woman who went ashore at the Argentine base at Esperanza. She wandered off on her own along the shore and somehow slipped and landed in a shallow pool of water. She was so heavy she was unable to get out. Eventually, one of the crewmen found her, and when he tried to lift her up she grabbed him around the neck in her desperation and brought him down with her and there the two lay floundering like stranded whales when the rest of us came along and saw the struggle. It took a great deal of strength to release her arms from around the unfortunate crewman, who by this time was almost crushed to death.

And then there was the very charming lady in her eighties who was extremely absentminded. She was obviously very wealthy, and she accompanied us on many cruises. What she derived from them was hard to imagine, as she very rarely went ashore, while spending a great deal of time at the bar. She could never remember the number of her cabin, so when about to turn in for the night she would simply go to the nearest cabin, open the door, and inquire, "Am I in the right place?" The other passengers came to know her well and had soon memorized the number of her cabin. It was a responsibility on board to lead her up to the right cabin. She was a charming old lady, a great flirt, and obviously in her early days had been extremely attractive. We were sitting at the bar once, and someone had invented a new drink. When we turned to her and remarked, "This will put hair on your chest," she responded, "I don't want any hair on my chest unless there's a head along with it."

Then there was the man who had some kind of mental problems. He was perfectly sane and pleasant during the day, but when he retired to his cabin he would become an entirely different person. One would hear screams of rage, shouting, and "arguments" coming from his cabin. It was only after a few days that we realized that he was not talking to any human companion, but perhaps to his shoes or some other item of apparel that was annoying him. He would get into a long argument talking to the inanimate object, whatever it was, and venting a great deal of anger upon it. His voice could be heard all up and down the alleyway as he raged.

I am convinced that an occasional elderly passenger is put aboard the ship by younger relatives in the hope that he will pass away on board and thus they will be rid of him, because in some cases we have had passengers who really did not know what they were in for or understand anything about the activities on board. There was one dear old gentleman on an Antarctic cruise who was convinced that he was on a train and kept insisting that he wanted to get off at the next station. We could not convince him otherwise.

And some people are so old and infirm that they are unable to go ashore at all, even under the most benign conditions. But perhaps they derived some pleasure on being in a congenial atmosphere, and everyone is extremely kind and considerate to them. Aside from such strange characters and the occasional complaining malcontent, the passengers on these expeditions are, in general, a splendid lot. Over the years, they return again and again. And these become like family members. We call them the repeaters, and many have become my very warm and close friends.

As for the staff, we have been through much together. The bonds are extremely close. There is a nucleus of lecturers, Zodiac handlers, and others working on the ship that have become the closest of friends. We have even organized our own society, SODS (Southern Ocean Drivers Society), including such fine people as Keith Shackleton, Alan Gurney, Jim Snyder, Mike McDowell, Tom Ritchie, and my son Peter. They are all highly skilled boatmen as well as superb naturalists. Over the years we have shared many exciting and sometimes droll experiences.

I recall, for instance, the rather difficult night at Cape Adare at the entrance to the Ross Sea in Antarctica.

We had landed the passengers on an open beach in fairly calm weather, so that they could visit a large Adélie penguin colony and also see the remarkable old hut, still standing and in good condition, erected by Carsten Borchgrevink in 1899, the first permanent structure ever to be erected on the Antarctic continent, with all the pieces fitted together in the Norwegian style without any nails or screws. It still stands there as a splendid example of a rugged little building. When it came time to get the passengers back on board, night had fallen, the wind had risen, and a heavy sea was breaking on the landing beach. We had to get the Zodiacs in as close as possible among the breakers, helping the passengers on board keep as dry as possible and getting the Zodiacs under way to the ship. We were standing waist-deep in the breakers to hold the Zodiacs in position while we got the passengers on board one by one. The wind was howling, and the water was vilely cold. But Pete had a bottle of Lambs Navy rum from the Falkland Islands, and this sustained us.

By the time the last passenger was brought safely on board, it was midnight, but we no longer felt like turning in. Possibly we were exhilarated by the excitement and difficulty we had undergone. The bar was open, hot-buttered rums were being served, and finally the passengers went to bed. But the SODS were in no mood to turn in. Someone put Handel's *Water Music* on the record player, and we took it in turns to conduct this inspiring music. Pretty soon we formed an orchestra; our instruments were invisible, but we played them with great verve and took our turns as conductors of this strange orchestra. When we had finished with Handel we went on to Beethoven's choral symphony, which also lent itself to our orchestral talents. So the night went on. Dawn came; a few early passengers entered the lounge, took one look at us, and without a word being spoken began performing on the instruments of their choice. While breakfast was in full swing, there we were, still at it. Since we had several days of open-sea cruising before we reached our next landing, we could afford to relax.

One of our SODS members deserves special mention. Jim Snyder became known an Unlucky Jim because of the series of disasters that always seemed to pick him out as their victim. A remarkably friendly, outgoing person, an extremely good photographer, and a good boatman, poor Jim was always having troubles. It is only necessary to cite a few of them to give the general picture. When Jim was running the Zodiacs, he would leave his camera equipment in the lobby until the passenger traffic to shore was over. Then he could retrieve his camera and use it to good effect. Unfortunately, he had the habit of wrapping it up in a dirty towel. At that time we had a particularly Amazonian type of hostess; Ruth was a strapping six-footer, and having spotted this bundle of dirty towel, she decided it was time it went to the laundry. The Chinese laundry is two flights of stairs down toward the bow. So she picked up the bundle and with a mighty heave sent Jim's camera, wrapped in its towel, down two flights of stairs, ending up, of course, looking more like a pretzel than a camera.

When we visited the organgutan rehabilitation center at Sepilok in Borneo we were watching the young orangs up in the trees coming down to accept bananas from us. As soon as they had a banana they would climb into the vines over our heads when one of them, feeling the need to relieve itself, let go. It is not necessary to say upon whose head the droplets fell.

The only time that Jim ever took the helm of the ship

was when we were in one of the lagoons in the Maldive Islands. The ship had almost come to a complete stop, and our captain, Hasse Nilsson, was on the bridge and he told Jim to take the wheel for a moment. Jim took the wheel and the next moment there was a crunch as the bow of the ship rammed a coral reef. Fortunately for the ship, at such a low speed the only damage was to that particular piece of coral, but it was just so appropriate that Jim was at the helm on that occasion, he was never allowed to forget it.

We were in the caldera on Deception Island with fairly pleasant weather, and the first Zodiac to be lowered was Jim's. Just as soon as he got into the water, up came one of these catabatic winds that are entirely unpredictable. With only Jim in the boat and having to be right in the stern with the engine, the catabatic caught the bow of the Zodiac and flipped it over, so Jim was in the water. He was able, of course, to climb out from the overturned Zodiac, and very soon there were other Zodiacs all around him to help get him aboard. The other Zodiac operators were given the task of retrieving all the floating equipment, such as paddles, cushions, and fuel tanks, out of Jim's Zodiac, and by the time they were through, they were all soaking wet from the howling squall. In the meantime Jim was drawn aboard soaking wet and immediately passengers were fussing over him, and he was ensconced with a large hot-buttered rum and a lot of sympathetic people all around him while his shipmates were still struggling to retrieve the capsized Zodiac and all its equipment. This was one time when Jim made out best.

Some of the beaches in South Georgia are becoming increasingly crowded by the growing population of fur seals, and at the time when we visit the island the reproductive cycle is well under way and the bulls are quite aggressive. To get the passengers to shore it is necessary for the staff to go ahead armed with canoe paddles or other weapons to fend off these belligerent animals to make a passage for the passengers so they can go inland. In Jim's case, he decided to go off with a couple of passengers who wished to visit some gray-headed albatross nests. So Jim landed on another beach where he encountered a very aggressive bull. Jim was fending off the seal with a Zodiac paddle when he slipped on a rock and fell face downward. In a moment the seal was on him and shook him like a terrier shaking a rat. Before help came, Jim had been severely bitten in the back and the thigh. It was fortunate that he had fallen facedown or the damage would have been more serious. As it was, when Jim was taken back to the ship it required the work of the ship's doctor to sew him up, and Jim required eighteen stitches in his back and a dozen more in his thigh.

On another occasion, Jim had hung out his rubber waders in the alleyway when a woman passenger suffering from an attack of seasickness passed by and was unable to contain herself any longer. Jim's boots caught the majority of the load.

There is no need to go into any more of Jim's misfortunes. Jim is a very likable fellow, and it does seem unfair that fate should have picked him out as the victim so many times. He also had trouble with various girlfriends, some of whom he brought on board, but fortunately I am now pleased to report that he is married and happily established, so it does not seem as though he will be back on board for a while.

13

Breaking the Ice with the Soviets

Of the more than 190 cruises I have made so far, the two I made in the summer of 1991 were the most exciting and unusual and deserve special mention. The ship was a recently built nuclear-powered Soviet icebreaker, the *Sovetskiy Soyuz* (Soviet Union). She was chartered by Salen Lindblad Cruising, a company I frequently work for, to make two cruises into the high Arctic. The first cruise was to reach the North Pole, the Transpolar Bridge, emerge from the far side, and end inside the Bering Strait. The second was to transit the Northeast Passage, from Bering Strait to Norway's North Cape, by way of the Siberian coast. The Soviet government, desperate for hard currency, particularly U.S. dollars, was pleased to accept the charter. So by late July, several other lecture staff members and I and eighty-six passengers, mostly American but some Europeans, assembled on the ship in Murmansk harbor.

Our first impressions were all favorable; the ship was clean, comfortable, and efficient. We were soon to learn of her impressive capabilities; her twin nuclear reactors gave her a maximum horsepower of 75,000 and a top speed in open water of twenty-two knots. Although with an overall length of 150 meters she was far larger than any of the other cruise ships I have worked on in the past, her passenger capacity was limited by the accommodations previously occupied by the ship's officers, who had temporarily moved into other quarters.

Sailing out of the Kola Fjord, we headed northward to a group of uninhabited islands known as the Franz Josef Land. Here we spent two and a half days, studying seabird colonies, botany, geology, and glaciology. We also found our first polar bears. Appropriately, it was our captain who spotted the first one; it was 2:00 A.M. when everyone was aroused by the loudspeaker system to see the animal as it slunk away, giving many backward glances at the ship pushing its way through the ice pack. No sooner were we back in our bunks again when another announcement brought us back on deck. This time no fewer than five animals were gathered around a bloody stain on the ice, where a bearded seal had been killed. Two of the bears, young adults, reluctantly backed off, but a mother with two half-grown cubs refused to leave, so the ship was able to move quietly within a hundred feet of the fascinating scene. Since broad daylight prevailed, there was a constant clicking of camera shutters for the next hour, while many yards of videotape were spinning off the reels.

On the fifth day in the pack we reached the geographic North Pole, the Transpolar Bridge, and after the captain had made some precise calculations to be certain that we were on the exact spot, a big champagne celebration was held. A barbecue was set up on a nearby floe, two poles were erected, and between them were flown the flags of all the nations represented by our shipmates. A few of us took a quick swim. There was a small patch of open water on the starboard side of the ship, so the gangway was lowered and we made the Polar Plunge, a very brief one, it must be admitted. When I emerged I was reminded of the story about the Scotsman who was skating on the ice when it gave way, and he remarked when he was hauled out he didn't know whether he was Angus or Agnes.

From then on we had a southward course, and on the tenth day we reached semiopen water in the vicinity of the New Siberian Islands, where an American expedition under the command of Lieutenant de Long in the *Jeannette* met its tragic end in 1879. The ship was crushed in the ice, and only a few survivors reached the Siberian mainland. When we neared Bennett Island one of the helicopters went in to make a reconnaissance and came back to report a sighting of a beach where about a thousand walrus were assembled, most on the beach but some in the water.

Since the coastline was ice-free, we could use the four Zodiacs to cruise close to shore, staying upwind of the walrus so we could drift quietly down toward them. But we soon found that these precautions were unnecessary. The animals showed no fear of us, and some swam within a few feet of the boats. There were many juveniles and some small babies, still nursing. Walrus are very sociable creatures; they like to lie huddled together, often with the youngsters piled on top. Those in the water were all around us; sometimes a large bull would come alongside in a semiaggressive manner, but we were never attacked. Groups of red-necked phalaropes were feeding on plankton along the water's edge, constantly bobbing their heads down to pick up tiny organisms.

When everyone had their encounters with the grotesque walrus, we cruised along some cliffs where there were teeming colonies of kittiwakes, thick-billed murres, and black guillemots, while glaucous gulls kept watch for untended eggs or chicks on which to prey. We also used the helicopters to land on another part of the island, where we found a sheltered area rich with small but beautiful Arctic wildflowers. The next day we visited Henrietta Island, but this time there was too much pack ice for the Zodiacs, so the helicopters were put into service again. We landed on a plateau and found several abandoned huts, but no sign of recent occupation. Many red phalaropes were nesting in this area; and when their nests were approached they put on a realistic "broken-wing" act in an attempt to lure us away.

Leaving this group of islands, we headed eastward for the pack ice around Wrangel Island, which is an important denning area for polar bears. More bears, including several mothers with cubs, and other wildlife were encountered here. We had hoped to make a landing on Wrangel, since it is noted for its abundant waterfowl and shorebird populations, and permission for a landing had already been granted by the Russian Republic State Committee for Environmental and Nature Preservation. The permission was overruled, however, by the Soviet government in Moscow, which voiced a strong objection to visits by groups of tourists. We contented ourselves, therefore, in circumnavigating this large island and its surrounding pack ice as we maintained a constant watch from the bridge for all forms of wildlife.

Crossing the Chuckchi Sea, we left the ice behind and began encountering gray whales in considerable numbers. They were feeding, taking in mouthfuls of bottom mud and water and straining it through their baleen plates for the invertebrates that were retained. As we entered Bering Straits and were in the Bering Sea we had gray whale spouts all around us, as these animals fattened up before returning to their long fasting period of mating and birthing in Mexican waters, during the late winter. Stops were made at several uninhabited islands to visit seabird colonies, walrus haul-out beaches, and rolling tundra rich with wildflowers, at their peak of blooming during the brief but extravagant Arctic summer.

The cruise ended at the small, drab port of Provideniya on the Siberian coast, and the passengers were flown to Anchorage in Alaska on a chartered flight. We had cruised a distance of 3,960 nautical miles in twenty-two days and had seen many parts of the world never before visited by tourists.

Two days later our next group of passengers arrived; many of them were veterans of the historic cruise we made on the *Lindblad Explorer* in 1984, when we were the first cruise vessel to make the transit of the Northwest Passage, from Newfoundland to Yokohama. Now they wanted to make the transit of the Northeast Passage from Bering Straits to Norway's North Cape. Among the passengers as my guest was my eldest granddaughter, Carin. Her enthusiasm and interest during the entire course of the cruise were a constant source of delight to me and to many others on board. In many aspects, this second cruise was the more interesting of the two, since we could make many more landings, see more wildlife, and meet more of the native people.

We made frequent stops along the Siberian coast. Due to her extreme draft (11.8 meters), it was often necessary for the ship to anchor many miles off the coast. Then, the helicopters served as ferries in a very casual but efficient way. Sometimes we were landed far inland, and once we visited a small community of Chuckchi people living in reindeer-skin tents in the rolling tundra. Their surprise must have been great to be suddenly surrounded by groups of red-jacketed foreigners coming out of the sky, but they gave us a warm welcome and were obviously delighted. The children were charming, and one little boy persuaded his even smaller brother to wear a pair of reindeer antlers so he could demonstrate his skills with a lasso.

Stopping at the southern islands of the New Siberian group, we were thrilled to find a pair of mammoth tusks protruding from the half-frozen clay cliffs. Along a beach we found another tusk sticking right out of the surf. No doubt there are many remains of these long-extinct animals in these seldom-visited islands. It was here, also, that we sighted several Ross's gulls, an elusive bird that breeds along parts of the Siberian coast and then seems to vanish to points unknown.

In late August the great upheaval was occurring in the Soviet government, and a coup d'état was attempted. The radio bulletins we were receiving on board were very disturbing, especially to the ship's officers, who feared a bloody revolution. When news came that the coup had collapsed we were all greatly relieved, and a big celebration was held, in which we all participated. When we visited the port of Pevek, we found that the Communist Party office was padlocked and the sign had been torn down. All the officers, who were reluctant party members, were then selling their membership cards to the passengers for $100 apiece as souvenirs, a very rapid switch to an entrepreneurial system. The generous tips in U.S. dollars that resulted from both cruises must have been rich rewards, shared by all the ship's crew. We learned that the chief engineer, with all his responsibilities, earned the equivalent of about $30 per month. The crew earned between $12 and $15 per month.

One of the big surprises for us was to find how suddenly Soviet paranoia and secrecy had changed to openness. A few years ago, anyone pointing a camera at a bridge or a railroad station or even a building would be asking for trouble. But on the ship, we were all offered tours, in small groups, of the reactor rooms, the control room, and the engine room, and we could take all the photographs we wanted. To visit the reactors, we were naturally required to wear protective clothing; everything was immaculately clean, and safety precautions appeared to be adequate. The reactors are the pressurized-water type. We were told that when the ship was going through heavy ice at the full 75,000 horsepower, 200 grams of enriched uranium was consumed in twenty-four hours. The ship can operate for four years before fuel replacement is necessary. The cast-steel prow is two meters thick at its strongest point, and the outer hull is fifty-five millimeters thick where ice is encountered and twenty-five millimeters thick elsewhere. The ice knife is located twenty-two meters aft of the prow. It is an outstanding paradox that this ship, so well designed, so ruggedly built, so admirably equipped and so competently operated, was the product of a nation teetering on the brink of collapse because of inefficiency, lethargy, and corruption.

We stopped for a couple of days at Franz Josef Island and then proceeded on to the longitude of the North Cape, to confirm the fact that we had made the transit of the Northeast Passage. Although the visibility was so poor we did not see the cape, even though it was only four miles away, we knew that we had succeeded, and a big celebration was held. The ship then turned back and headed for Murmansk, which we reached the following morning.

The two cruises were over, and all our objectives had been attained. For the Soviet officers and crew, the passengers, and the lecture staff, the cruises had been a unique experience and, from every viewpoint, an outstanding success. We had reached the pole, we had traveled the Northeast Passage, and we had encountered much wildlife and interesting people, in the parts of the world never before seen by tourists. Moreover, we had established warm and lasting friendships with our fine Soviet shipmates on a superb ship. In other words, and in more senses than one, we had broken the ice with the Soviets.

I had another experience with a Russian icebreaker in the summer of 1993. This was the diesel-powered *Kapitan Khlebnikov*, chartered by Quark Expeditions of Darien, Connecticut, in an attempt to circumnavigate Greenland. This had never been done, and the ice around northern Greenland has the reputation of being some of the world's toughest. We had ninety-three passengers, mostly Americans but some Europeans.

We started in mid-August, when conditions are most suitable and new ice is not forming to any great extent. Our starting point was Sondrestrom Fjord, on Greenland's southwest coast, and from there we proceeded on a counterclockwise course, stopping at small fishing communities and also visiting Bratthalid, to see the remains of the Viking settlement established by Eric the Red over one thousand years ago. Proceeding up the east coast, we made stops at the attractive little town of Angmagssalik and several other fjords. Halfway up the east coast we explored the extensive fjords of Scoresby Sound, where we stalked a herd of musk oxen.

At this point we began encountering extensive fields of pack ice, and the ice maps we received on the ship's fax machine indicated heavy concentrations in the Greenland Sea, in the northeast. So we decided to abandon the original plan to explore more fjords and head nonstop for the north coast as fast as we could, to give us some days in hand. All went well as we had Cape Morris Jessup abeam. This is Greenland's northernmost point. The two ship's helicopters were able to land us on a pebble beach, where a small refuge hut and an unmanned weather hut with automated instrumentation stood.

Proceeding westward from there, the going became increasingly slow and difficult. Ice cover now was over nine-tenths, meaning there was very little space between the floes. Morever, this was multiyear ice, making it extremely tough; it would not split when attacked and was over two meters thick. In the meantime, we received advice from a Canadian icebreaker that the Robeson Channel, between Ellesmere Island and northwest Greenland, was entirely blocked with large floes of multiyear ice. They told us that there was absolutely no possibility of our ship, with her 22,000 horsepower, breaking through. By this time, the ice field had drifted in around us, so our route back eastward was also cut off. The ship could not move, either forward or back.

We were beset.

Fortunately, the *Yamal*, one of the latest Russian nuclear-powered icebreakers, was returning from a cruise to the North Pole, heading for Murmansk. By making a slight deviation from her original course, she would be able to reach us in several days. So we waited, entertaining our passengers with helicopter flights, lectures, and videos. Early on the morning of September 4, *Yamal* was sighted in the distance, slowed down to three knots at times. She had to contend with many pressure ridges, requiring all her 72,000 horsepower to ram her way through. When at last she reached us, a gangway was rigged between the two ships, so we could visit back and forth and exchange experiences. *Yamal* is sister ship to the *Sovetskiy Soyuz*, on which I reached the North Pole in 1991.

We then followed eastward in *Yamal*'s wake for over a hundred miles. Even she, with all her power, had to back up and ram forward again and again to break through. Both captains claimed they had never encountered so much tough multiyear ice.

Finally free, we headed for Svalbard (Spitsbergen), where we had five days to explore this magnificent area, which I have visited many times on *Polaris*. Here, we were able to land on Kvitoya (White Island), a desolate, frozen spot where the bodies of the three members of the ill-fated Andree Balloon Expedition were found thirty-two years after their balloon came down on the pack ice in 1898. We also had sightings of polar bears, walrus, and other wildlife. There was much splendid glacier scenery to enjoy.

So, although we had not succeeded in circumnavigating Greenland, our passengers were good sports and agreed that the exciting experiences had been worth it, and the cruise ended on an upbeat thanks to the splendors of the Svalbard archipelago.

14

Memories

One of our most memorable parties was held at Port Stanley in the Falkland Islands on the New Year's Eve following the conflict between Argentina and Great Britain. Ours was the first nonmilitary vessel to visit the islands following the war, and our ship was able to contribute, with liquor and appetizers, to the grand party to be held at Government House. In the meantime a huge bonfire had been prepared up the hill behind Government House, and at the stroke of midnight the fire was lit and all military vessels in the harbor began firing tracers and rockets. A blaze began and we all assembled around this great fire to celebrate the outcome of the conflict. It was a heartwarming experience, for there was no one in the Falklands who wanted to be under the control of Argentina. So there was great cause to celebrate.

Our host was, naturally, Sir Rex Hunt, governor of the islands at that time. He is a man I very much admire, for he stood up to the Argentines and refused to shake hands with the general of the invading forces. In fact, he should probably go down in history as being responsible for one of those timeless statements, such as, "Fire when ready," or, "Don't give up the ship." When the Argentine navy came steaming into Port Stanley, on the day of the invasion, Sir Rex turned around to an aide and said, "I think the silly buggers really mean it this time." In any case this party, which began at Government House, then moved to the bonfire and eventually to our little ship, where it continued well on into the following morning.

Another occasion outstanding in our memories was a nightmare of a night spent in the Kerguelen islands. These inhospitable, windswept, desolate islands in the Southern Ocean were on the itinerary for a long cruise that started in Singapore and was programmed to end in Tierra del Fuego. The problem for this particular voyage was the fact that the ship was unable to carry sufficient fuel for the entire cruise, so some had been shipped in advance to the French base in the Kerguelens at Port Au Français, where we were to refuel. On arriving there we found that the fuel had arrived, but the only way we could get it aboard was by means of a hose line that had to be laid from the shore, supported by floats, to the ship. One of the problems in landing on this island was the great masses of kelp close to the shore, a trap for the Zodiacs because of the entanglement of the propellers. It was blowing a howling gale, but we somehow managed to get the pipeline to the ship and began filling our tanks. But for the Zodiac drivers it was indeed a nightmare. There were very few lights on shore, and Keith Shackleton in one Zodiac became so entrapped he was unable to get out until the following morning; he had to spend the night on the beach. Fortunately, he found a small cabin where he could take shelter. The other Zodiacs also got entangled in the kelp and required help to get free. It was a night that none of us will ever forget.

On one of the longer Antarctic cruises where my son Peter and I were crowded into a cabin down in the bow, in an area known as Chinatown, because of its proximity to the Chinese laundry, Pete was still out carousing with some of the crew. But I had turned in early. We were in Antarctica's Ross Sea, bucking into a force-twelve gale, which means winds of hurricane force of over sixty knots, and the ship was pitching wildly, emphasizing the motion at the bow end of the vessel. I was in the lower of a two-bunk metal framework bolted to the wall when, in an extra-steep pitch, the bolts pulled out of the wall. The entire contraption was surging back and forth in the cabin with me struggling to hold it in one place just as Pete came in to this surprising scene. He disappeared immediately to find a rope to secure the lively monster before damage was done.

Another memorable experience of an entirely different kind must be recounted. Cruising in Arctic waters along the coast of Baffin Island, we came to an enormous colony of a seabird known as the thick-billed murre. This is a type of auk that raises its single chick on a ledge on the face of vertical cliffs. When the chick is still only half-fledged, it is persuaded by the male parent to leap from these high ledges. One would think that most of the chicks would perish in this way, by being battered on the rocks below if they were not fortunate enough to land in the sea. Their wings are still too rudimentary to be of much use to them in making these jumps, sometimes from a good many hundreds of feet. But the little creatures seem to be made of rubber. They have a fatty pad on their breasts and can actually bounce on the rocks, and so the only ones that perish are those that land in crevasses out of which they cannot extricate themselves. The male parent leads the chick down, and as soon as it reaches the water it is led off to sea and the father begins showing it how to dive. The female parent remains at her little spot of real estate on the ledge where she hatched her chick and maintains this off and on for the next couple of weeks, thus reinforcing her territorial rights to this particular spot for the following year. The father, in the meantime, accompanies the chick where it is relatively safe from predation from glaucous gulls, great black-backed gulls, and skuas.

One is obliged to wonder why the chick does not wait until its wings are fully developed so that it can fly when it first leaves its nest site. But this means of survival makes perfectly good sense. The fact is that by the time the chick is half-fledged, its appetite is so enormous that both parents must obtain food for it, instead of one being able to remain behind to protect it. If unprotected, it would become vulnerable as a tasty mouthful to the predatory birds that are always hanging around a big colony like this. The jumps of these little birds generally occur in the late evening, when the chances of predation are somewhat reduced.

On one occasion we happened to be at the right spot at the right time, and the captain was able to edge the ship right in under the cliffs, so we could watch, under ideal conditions, a shower of these chicks coming down with their fathers in close attendance. It was a thrilling sight; a few of these little creatures actually landed on the foredeck, where they were, of course, immediately tossed into the water to come under the charge of their fathers. This was another of the many unforgettable memories that are still as fresh as the day on which they occurred.

And what could be more moving than to be able to sit beside a royal albatross as she covers her single chick? On the final Antarctic cruise of the season, when we make the long voyage around the continent to the Ross Sea and finish the voyage in New Zealand before heading up for the tropics, we stop at some of the Antarctic islands on the New Zealand side. One of these is Campbell Island, where there is a scattered colony of the royal albatross.

This, along with the wandering albatross, is the largest flying bird, with a wingspan of well over eleven feet. Both the royal and the wandering albatross show absolutely no fear of man. One can even gently reach under their bodies to touch the egg or chick.

It sometimes happens that on approaching one of these birds it will rise to its feet as if to present its chick to the unexpected visitor. It will look down at the chick and then at you and then will settle down again on its nest. I can find no other explanation for this very touching example of pride and faith but that it is showing off its offspring to one whom it considers an appreciative visitor. Perhaps I sound unduly sentimental, but I cannot help becoming somewhat anthropomorphic at such times.

The penguin colonies are always a source of entertainment. To sit at the edge of a penguin colony and watch the constant activities is a source of endless interest. Adélie penguins in particular, with their quizzical, clownlike expressions, their flippers sometimes extended to add to their indication of astonishment, are indeed droll. We must remember, however, that the penguin's life is far from a comedy, however comical they may appear to us. Their adapting and succeeding in such a harsh environment is a tribute to their marvelous struggle for survival. They could not have succeeded had they not been able to adapt to these harsh conditions: the deadly cold water, battering surf, and predations by skuas, leopard seals, and killer whales, and yet there they are in Antarctica in their millions. Their close-packed colonies have some of the aspects of a noisy and somewhat unsanitary town. To keep their eggs and chicks out of the melting snow, they build nests out of little stones, the only material available to them. To obtain these stones they become thieves. The thefts go on continuously; any nest that is unprotected, even for a few moments, is victimized. On one occasion, a late snowfall had half-buried the female as she was incubating her eggs, so just her head protruded above the snow. Her devoted husband, in the meantime, was stealing stones from another nest, but since he could not deposit them in the nest itself, he would place them at the edge of the hole from which her head protruded. As soon as his back was turned, however, another penguin standing nearby and gazing off, apparently innocently into space, would turn around and quickly seize one of the stones and take it off to his own nest. This little comedy went on as I watched for several hours. The faithful husband, not being anything of a mathematician, was never aware of the fact that his little pile of stones was not growing. The female, as soon as the theft occurred, would extend her head as much as possible and, obviously using bad penguin language, object to the theft. But she could not reach the thief, and so the comedy continued unabated.

As the chicks grow older they leave the nest site and form crèches, huddling together in tight masses. As soon as they are in a crèche, which would indicate that they are in good condition, the skuas will not bother them. But if a chick wanders off on its own, it is likely to be seized by a skua, dragged out of the colony, and killed. The parent will feed no other chick but its own, and how they are able to recognize the voice of their chick out of the thousands all around is hard to understand, yet somehow they do. As the chick gets larger and larger, instinct compels the adult to begin exercising the chick in the only way possible to prepare it for the tough life ahead. This is done by deliberately running away from the chick before delivering its food. It is a comical sight to see an adult pursued by one or sometimes both chicks,

222

running all through the colony while the chicks, peeping desperately, keep falling in their clumsy way, becoming spattered with mud and other unspeakable materials, until eventually the parent will relent and turn around to regurgitate the semidigested food. But by this time nobody but a mother could love the repellent-looking off-spring, grossly fat and covered with all kinds of filth.

The king penguin's reproductive cycle is quite re-markable. If they are successful, they can produce two chicks within a three-year cycle, the development of the chick taking many months. When the female lays the egg, she incubates it for a few hours and then departs to feed at sea, having lost about a quarter of her body weight during the three weeks of courtship and laying. The male has also been fasting during courtship, and he takes over the incubation when the female leaves by placing the egg on his feet and covering it with a loose flap of skin on the lower part of his body. He will stand there with the egg on his feet for about nineteen days, losing up to 30 percent of his body weight. The female, when she returns, will incubate for a similar long period. The male then leaves her for about twelve days, and the egg usually hatches when the female returns after about five days, the total incubation period being around fifty-five days. The chick continues to be brooded while small under this flap of skin on the lower body, but once the chick is hatched, the parents alternate every few days. It is remarkable that these birds are able to build up sufficient reserves of met-abolic fat on which they can subsist during the incuba-tion period.

In the case of the larger emperor penguin, however, the process is even more extraordinary. The emperor pen-guin breeds on the sea ice during the Antarctic winter, and this often requires traveling seventy or eighty miles in the heart of the Antarctic winter into the interior, where the courtship takes place. Once the egg is laid the female returns to the sea, having lost about 20 percent of her body weight. The egg rests on the feet of the male for the entire incubation period, which, as it is such a large egg, requires about sixty-five days. This occurs in the heart of the Antarctic winter, with total darkness, howling gales, and temperatures going down to as much as minus seventy degrees Fahrenheit. The males huddle together as best they can to conserve as much body heat as possible. If all has gone well with the female, she will return just about the time that the egg hatches and is then able to feed the chick.

If, however, by some mishap the female does not return, perhaps having fallen prey to a killer whale or leopard seal, a male can still produce from an esophageal gland an exudate full of protein to provide the chick with its first meal, this in spite of the fact that the male is emaciated by this time, having lost almost one-half of his body weight. This extraordinary reproductive cycle was hard for the early explorers to believe, but in view of the long incubation period and the long period required by the chick to develop, it is necessary for the egg to be laid in the heart of the Antarctic winter. By the time the chick is fledged in late November or December, the sea ice is beginning to break up, so the journeys of the penguins between their chicks and the sea are much shortened. By the time the chick is ready to go, it has its own ice floe from which it can take off. I have suggested that members of women's lib organizations adopt the emperor penguins as their official bird.

Aside from the penguins, one of the most delightful birds in the Antarctic is the cape petrel or cape pigeon or pintado, as the early sealers and whalers called it. It is a lovely little black and white bird with a checkerboard pattern on its back. It is one of the first Antarctic seabirds to greet us as we cross the Convergence. The pintados appear in considerable numbers around the ship and escort us for hours at a time, flying not only behind the stern, but alongside our vessel. They remind me of the small boys accompanying the circus parade into town, as there seems to be no other answer for it but the enjoyment of accompanying us. They are very abundant and nest in ledges in the rocks. As they show no fear of man at all when on their nests, it is possible to approach within a couple of feet of them without them showing any sign of disturbance. A bird returning to its nest is greeted by its mate with musical chatterings that continue some time before they settle down together.

The elephant seals also provide great entertainment and interest. These enormous mammals drag themselves out onto the beaches and pile up together like gigantic sausages, grunting and making vulgar bathroom sounds as they roll over. When approached closely, they will show their displeasure by opening their large pink mouths but otherwise do not show signs of aggression. Occasionally a couple of young bulls will spar together by rearing up the front part of their bodies and battering each other with their chests, giving out great belching sounds. This will go on for a few minutes, and then suddenly they will flop over and go back to sleep. During molting, the fur comes off in small patches and it is obvious that this is a very irritating period for the animals, as they are constantly scratching with their short front flippers. They have a very motheaten look at this period, with loose patches of yellowish brown fur on various parts of their bodies.

Yet these monsters that look so awkward and clumsy on land are superb deep-sea divers, and recent study indicates that they are able to dive to depths of several thousand feet without any problems. How they are able to locate the squid and fish on which they feed is still a mystery, but they are extremely efficient in the water. It is only rarely that one sights an elephant seal at sea. They are nearly always down below, where they are safe from killer whales and sharks, which do not go down to these abyssal depths.

In the early summer of 1978 we suffered a deep, irreparable loss. Our oldest son, Dennis Edward, was atop El Castillo, Chichén Itzá, in Yucatán, Mexico, when he was struck by a bolt of lightning and killed instantly. His two children, Cedric (nine) and Lyda (six), were at a lower level. At that time, Denny was an associate professor of anthropology at the University of Minnesota, conducting research in Maya archaeology and agriculture. He had become deeply interested in Maya religion, exploring the underground rivers in Belize believed to be the passages to Xibalba, the lowest level of the Maya underworld. There is much local superstition that his utterly unexpected and dramatic death was due to the gods' taking him for their own. His brief, brilliant career was responsible for many innovative theories about Maya subsistence, and a conference on that subject was held in his memory on October 4, 5, and 6, 1979, at the University of Minnesota.

One does never completely recover from a loss of that magnitude.

15

Conclusion—Not Quite

And so the memories pile up, and I wonder when the reservoir will overflow and some will be lost, although this does not seem to have happened yet. While possibly some become a little misted by time, they can still be recalled on demand with some effort and in great clarity by the brain, that extraordinary repository of experiences from the past. Now close to ninety, I presume before long I will be obliged to put an end to all this adventuring and collapse into the nearest wheelchair. Then I can begin in earnest living again through all those marvelous years, instead of looking toward the future as I do now. Whatever the future brings me, I can claim with great sincerity to have been blessed as have few others. Not only do I belong to a close and loving family, but furthermore, I am rich in my many good friends, as well as being in excellent health, and I have been able to nurture and expand my other loves. There is the sea, in all its moods and with all the islands and coastlines it embraces. Once it was for me an implacable enemy, ready to destroy me if I relaxed my guard. But when I consider all that it has brought me it becomes a friend of inestimable worth. And the birds, with their reminders of lives that are totally innocent and unblemished by so many of mankind's regrettable traits. In their grace, mobility, and elegance they have been my constant inspiration and delight.

I have only to close my eyes, shut off extraneous sounds, and here the memories come passing before me in an endless parade: the faint loom of a distant island as it emerges from the horizon under the wind-taut curve of the staysail after a thirty-day open-sea passage; an estimated two thousand beluga whales churning the waters of the Churchill River in Hudson Bay; the coast of remote Zavodovski Island in the South Sandwich group, where an estimated 18 million chinstrap penguins were breeding, while inland from them a great active volcanic crater was spewing out ashes and smoke in the evening air; the haunting call of a curlew bubbling to a crescendo as it speaks to its mate of the eggs that are its ultimate treasure; the great barnacle-encrusted head of a gray whale resting on the side of my Zodiac, ready to be petted in an inexplicable communication between man and cetacean; on Komodo Island in Indonesia, watching the formidable eleven-foot monitor lizards known as Komodo dragons tearing apart the carcass of a goat; the sight of one-half million puffins swarming in the air like gigantic bumblebees on a desolate island off the north coast of Norway, with thousands more resting on the water; the soft notes of a guitar combining with the rustling of palm fronds stirred by the breeze, heard across a Pacific lagoon at twilight; the sight at a distance of ninety miles of the great ice-capped volcanic cone of Beerenberg Mountain on lonely Jan Mayen Island, sparkling in the early-morning sun; the shimmering, iridescent plumage of that masterpiece of ornithological brilliance, the golden-headed quetzal, as it roosts sedately in the lush Venezuelan cloud forest; the voice of ancient glacial ice as I sit silently in a boat in Antarctica's Paradise Bay surrounded by brash whispering as the trapped air bubbles escape with a gentle crackling; and the wandering albatross soaring effortlessly in our ship's wake as we cruise the Southern Ocean. Is it the same bird that has been attached to us by an invisible bond for the past few days? I like to think so. All these memories and thousands more are the riches I have amassed in my lifetime. Is there anyone who is richer?